"Do I pass muster one eyebrow.

Liza snapped her attention back to the present. "I'm sorry?"

"You're staring."

She swallowed her disappointment. For a moment, she had expected him to be his old self again, holding out his hands to her and smiling. The new Matthew did not behave like that.

Sorrow for the loss filled her, something precious as gold slipping through her fingers. If ever he loved her, that part of him was forgotten. Maybe he'd never loved her at all. How could she tell?

"Yes, it'll do." She hefted the basket with her shopping, but he slipped it out from her grasp. He offered her his left arm, escorting her down Main Street for all the world as if he were promenading down the finest street in St. Louis on a Sunday afternoon. Despite her sadness, she spared a moment to be amused by his air. He had always treated her like a rare precious object. Right up to the point he had left.

According to family tradition, **Evelyn M. Hill** is descended from a long line of horse thieves. (But when your family is both Texan *and* Irish, tall tales come with the territory.) That might explain why she grew up writing horse stories. These days, the stories feature a handsome cowboy, as well. She lives at the end of the Oregon Trail, where she gets to do her historical research in person.

Books by Evelyn M. Hill

Love Inspired Historical

His Forgotten Fiancée

EVELYN M. HILL

His Forgotten Fiancée

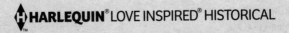

Recycling programs
for this product may
not exist in your area.

LOVE INSPIRED BOOKS

ISBN-13: 978-1-335-36952-9

His Forgotten Fiancée

33614080499709

www.Harlequin.com

Printed in U.S.A.

For now we see through a glass, darkly; but then face to face: now I know in part; but then shall I know even as also I am known.
—*1 Corinthians* 13:12

For the two Kit Carsons in my life,
blazing a trail for the rest of us.

Chapter One

"Who am I?"

Liza Fitzpatrick dropped the cleaning rag onto the counter of the dry goods store and spun around. A man stood in the doorway, his rough, working-class clothes soaked through. He was staring at her as if she were the first woman he'd ever seen.

Ten steps to the back room, half a minute to grab Pa's rifle. She might be able to make it. Sober, the long-legged man could easily outpace her. But not the way he was swaying from side to side. It was getting dark outside, and she found it difficult to guess his age in the light from the single lantern, but beneath the beard and the bedraggled brown hair that fell to his shoulders, he looked under thirty.

"Well?" Impatience edged his tone like a well-honed knife.

She cleared her throat. "Um…good evening. Mr. Vandehey, three doors down, serves liquor—"

"That's the last thing I need." He sagged against the door frame, his head drooping.

She took a couple of cautious steps closer, to get a better look at the man. Red streaks trailed down his forehead. "You're hurt!"

His head came up. "Obviously." Those thick eyebrows could have been designed to scowl at her. His dark eyes woke the memory of a pain that she had thought buried safely away. Recognition twisted inside her like a knife plunged straight into her heart. He said, "Do you know who I am?"

"You don't know?" She stared at him. This encounter was starting to take on the unreal qualities of a nightmare. That was ironic, considering she had been dreaming of this moment for months. She had imagined all the different ways the scene would play out—or she thought she had.

"I am trying to be patient, madam." The man spoke with a cultured accent at odds with his wild mountain-man appearance. "I would appreciate the courtesy of an answer to my one—simple—question. Do you know who I am?"

"Yes," she said. "You are the man I am going to marry."

He swayed against the door frame, sliding slowly down to the ground in a faint.

Liza had thought she would never see him again.

She looked down at the man sprawled on the floor. His eyes were shut, dark lashes long against his pale skin. Liza had a thousand questions that needed answers, but now was not the time, not when Matthew Dean lay passed out at her feet.

Her emotions were in a whirl. She had been waiting for this day for over a year, hoping for it, praying for it, sometimes almost dreading it. And now that he had finally come back to her, it didn't seem real. She crouched down, pushing up his sleeve to put her fingers against his wrist. His skin was cold, but his pulse beat strongly against her hand. For a moment he responded to her touch, his fingers curving to grasp her hand. He murmured something under his breath, and then his hand drooped.

She didn't know whether she should laugh or cry. He had been gone for so long, without a word. Why had he come back now?

Her mother had always told her that the Lord never sent you anything unless He had faith in your ability to withstand it. Sometimes, she wished the Lord didn't have quite so much faith in her.

She fetched Jim Barnes from the livery stable on the corner to help her get the unconscious man into the bed in the back room. Jim cleaned him up while Liza dug up some dry clothes. Mr. McKay, the owner of the dry goods store, was shorter and much wider, but his homespun trousers and red-checked shirt would have to do. Matthew's clothes weren't merely damp, they were soaked through. She rubbed the rough, sodden fabric between her fingers, then spread the clothes out by the fireplace in the front room. They hadn't had rain in weeks. He must have fallen into the river to get this wet.

Jim came out of the back room, shutting the door quietly behind him. "Restless man, won't hardly lie still," he said. "Like there's something burning a hole in him."

"How badly is he hurt? Memory loss sounds pretty serious. I should probably send for the doctor." She frowned, torn between worry and frustration.

"Doc Graham won't be back until tomorrow, but I don't think he's in bad shape," Jim reassured her. "Just that cut on his head, which has already stopped bleeding. Looks like he got roughed up some, is all."

"I appreciate your help." Liza hesitated. Jim, placid and unflappable, had accepted her explanation that the man was her fiancé without any questions. But other people would be more curious, asking questions she did not know the answers to. *I need to know where I stand. I need to know why he came back after all this time.* "I'd appreciate it if you did not mention this incident to anyone. Not tonight."

He gave her a look that was unexpectedly shrewd. "Anyone like Mr. Brown, you mean? I won't say a word to him about it, but I'll send Granny Whitlow over to keep you company. Wouldn't be proper, otherwise."

Matthew was hardly in a position to pose a threat to any woman at the moment, but Liza nodded. "Thank you, Jim."

After he left, she began to tidy up, sweeping the floor and straightening the goods on the shelves.

The dry goods store was the front room of the McKays' home. It still had the original puncheon floor and the cat-and-clay fireplace that was used for cooking and to heat the house, but the walls were filled with shelves of nails, rope and harnesses, as well as the latest bolts of fabric off ships from Boston and New York. The back room was the family's private area, and the children slept up in the loft. Liza had agreed to mind the store for the McKays when they went upriver to Champoeg to celebrate their eldest son's wedding.

It was getting late, but she could not close up the store yet; there was one more visitor coming to see her tonight. She was already dreading it. Meeting with Mr. Brown was never pleasant.

It was possible that no one had noticed Matthew's arrival tonight. There were a lot of strangers in town these days. In the year since Liza had come, the town of Oregon City had doubled in size. More people were coming in from the trail each week, making their way around Mount Hood on the Barlow Road or risking the passage down the Columbia River past The Dalles, all eager to claim land.

She recognized that longing; it was what had led her and her pa to take the Oregon Trail. It was all she had ever wanted since she was a child—a place she could call her own. No one to look down on her for being the daughter of an Irish immigrant. Here, they were all immigrants together. This was a place where she could put down roots. She could have a family— She winced away from the thought. It led back to the man lying unconscious in the bed in the other room.

It had been almost a year since she'd last seen him. Perhaps he had an explanation for what he'd done. Perhaps he had come to apologize.

The front door opened. Old Granny Whitlow stomped in, bringing a rush of cool evening air with her. "What's this I hear? Some man barged in here?" She looked around. "Where's he now, then? Don't just stand there, girl!"

"He's resting. I don't want to disturb him." Liza shut the door behind Granny. She only wished she could close the door on this conversation, as well. She had wanted a chance to talk to Matthew privately first.

"Humph." Granny did not look impressed. As one of the founding members of the Ladies' Social Club, she seemed to feel it was her duty to collect and spread the latest news among the townspeople. "I was hoping to get a look at the fella."

"He's been injured," Liza said. "There's really no need for you to stay. He's not going to hurt me."

The dry goods store served as the social center for the women of the town, so Mrs. McKay had placed a couple of rocking chairs by the fire for visitors, and a table with Mr. McKay's prized chess set on it. Granny settled herself in one of the rocking chairs and then looked up at Liza. "You sound pretty certain about a total stranger."

"He's not a stranger. His name is Matthew Dean. I don't want Mr. Brown to know he's here, not until

I've had a chance to talk to Matthew, but..." Liza's voice trailed off. This was harder than she had expected. She had to force the words out. "He's the man I got betrothed to on the trail."

The silence was so profound that she could hear the tinny piano being played all the way down in Vandehey's saloon.

"Well, if that don't beat all. You've been refusing offers left and right on account of your being promised to some man none of us have ever seen, and here he pops up all out of nowhere." Granny nodded her head.

Liza felt her cheeks growing warm. "When he went off down the California Trail instead of coming on to Oregon with me, he promised he'd come up once he'd gotten a stake, and then we'd get married. It just took longer than I thought, that's all."

"Months and months. California's full of them pretty Spanish girls, I do hear."

"He loves me." Was she trying to convince the other woman or herself? Liza shoved that thought aside. "He asked me to marry him, and he's an honorable man."

"Humph. Men change their minds just as much as women do. If he was coming up here to marry you and all, why was he down there all that time and never sent you a letter?" Granny spoke triumphantly, hammering the final nail in the coffin.

Every word she said was true, but Liza didn't want to hear it all the same. "He asked me to marry him. He promised he'd come back to me. Now he has."

Granny said skeptically, "And he just happened to wander straight to your door? Just you go and fetch those quilts from up in the loft. I can't manage that ladder, but no matter. I'll be comfy as anything right here in this chair for the night."

Liza got a couple of quilts for herself as well, spreading one across the other rocking chair. "Anyone in town knows I've been minding the dry goods store while the McKays are upriver. He could have been given directions here before he was injured." Granny still looked skeptical. "And, of course, this was the only place still open, apart from the saloon."

"You really shouldn't keep the store open this late. I'll help you put up the shutters."

"No." Liza put out a hand to stop her. "I can't close up the store yet. I'm waiting for someone."

Granny narrowed her eyes. "At this hour? Who?"

As Liza started to answer, the door was pushed open again. The man in the doorway was of medium height, slim, with brown hair and a neatly trimmed mustache. There was nothing remarkable about his appearance, but dread curled into a knot in Liza's stomach. "Good evening, Mr. Brown."

"Good evening." He nodded to Granny. "Mrs. Whitlow." He paused. "Might I speak with you privately, Miss Fitzpatrick? Perhaps we could use the other room. There is a matter I would like to discuss with you."

"No," Liza said quickly. "We can talk here. It is all right if Granny stays."

"Don't mind me," Granny said brightly. "I'll be quiet as a mouse." She folded her hands, eyes bright with curiosity.

Liza went behind the counter, where she had her reticule waiting. "I have the money here." She handed him the coins. It was almost all the money she had in the world, but giving it to him was worth the sacrifice if that meant keeping the claim. "There. That is the last payment. Now Pa does not owe you anything, and neither do I."

Mr. Brown put his wallet away inside his jacket. He withdrew a piece of paper. "And here is the IOU. It was unfortunate that your pa needed to borrow money, but I'm glad at least that I was able to be the one to help you in your time of need."

"Thank you." She had to force the words out. "I am sure Pa thought he was doing the best he knew how, but I would prefer if he did not borrow money from anyone in the future. I can take care of him until he gets on his feet again." *And next time, he can* tell *me when he borrows money to keep the claim going.*

"Can you?" The question was mild, but those pale green eyes were intent upon her. "Apparently, you have not heard. Your hired hands quit this afternoon." His thin lips curved up into a faint smile. "They should be halfway to Astoria by now."

The words settled into her like lead weights. "I expect we'll manage." She only wished she knew how. There was no way she could get the harvest in by herself.

"It looks like you've gotten some new supplies." Mr. Brown scanned the bolts of fabric on the shelf behind her. "I'd like a few yards of that braided trim if you would be so kind."

Liza measured out the yards of fabric and wrapped it up for him. He was playing with her, wasting her time. What use did a man have for trimming? None.

He never shifted his gaze from her. "You could sell the claim to the Baron, you know." Mr. Brown's boss, Barclay Hughes, had come out to the Oregon Territory a few years back. He had quickly made a fortune cutting down trees and shipping the wood down to San Francisco. To his face, everyone called him Mr. Hughes. Behind his back, he was known as the Baron. "He wants the land. He'll be pleased if I can get it for him. I can make sure that he doesn't cheat you on the deal. He listens to me. He will give you a good price for your claim, and you could find permanent work in town."

"Sell the claim? And give up our independence? Thank you all the same, but no. My father is going to prove up his claim, and I am going to help him. No one is going to take it from us." She finished wrapping up the fabric and pushed it across the counter to him.

Mr. Brown leaned forward, and she had to repress the urge to step back. "Frankly, Miss Fitzpatrick, you can't do it. Not just you and your father."

He thought she would give in. Thought she had no choice.

Since that tree had fallen on Pa's legs, breaking them both, getting the crops in had become a major worry in her life. Without the harvest, she and Pa would not be able to afford to stay on the claim over the winter, which meant they would lose it. The law specified a man had to live on his claim if he wanted to prove it.

The wheat was ripe now. There was no time to hunt for new helpers. If she put off the harvest, the rains would come and the crops would rot in the fields.

Her thoughts flitted to the man in the back room. Mr. Brown had always acted possessive where she was concerned, no matter how often she'd made it clear that she had no interest in him. Dealing with him had been awkward enough when she had only been paying off Pa's IOU. Once he learned that her fiancé was in town, it would be a thousand times worse.

She couldn't face his reaction to the news. Not tonight, when she was still trying to come to terms with Matthew being back in her life. Perhaps by morning, Matthew would remember who he was, who she was. What they had meant to each other. All she knew for sure at this moment was that she needed to talk to him before she could decide how to handle Mr. Brown's reaction to the news. She went to the front door and held it open. "Please don't let me keep you."

"I'll talk to you tomorrow, when you've had more time to consider. I know you're a stubborn little lady, but I'm sure by morning you'll understand that I only want what is best for you."

From her place by the fire, Granny called out, "You'll be wanting to go back to the hotel before you lose your chance of supper. I don't know why you don't just board with some respectable family instead of paying all that money to stay at that fancy new place, but that's young men for you. Always have to present a good image to the world."

Mr. Brown opened his mouth to speak, then he shut it again, pressing his lips together. Anger stained his cheeks with bright red patches. Abruptly, he turned and left.

Liza shut the door behind him and bolted it. She leaned against it, closing her eyes for a moment, and a sigh escaped her.

"There's a man who dearly likes to get his own way." Granny's dry voice came from behind her. "Mr. Brown won't be happy until he's gotten your claim for the Baron."

"That's what I am afraid of." Liza sat down in the other rocking chair and wrapped the quilt tightly around herself. "I don't know what to do about the harvest." There. She had said it out loud.

"Why is that man so set on your claim? He's bought up most of the claims around. You'd think he'd be satisfied."

She shook her head. "He wants to please the Baron. He thinks if he goes through me, Pa will agree to sell the claim."

"That's true enough. Whole town knows your pa would do anything for you."

"*For* me, yes." It never occurred to him to let her share the burden. That was part of the problem. Granny was looking at her, eyebrows raised, so Liza explained further. "After my mother's death, Pa left me with my aunt in Iowa while he came out here and threw all his energy into building a new home for us on the claim. I think it helped him deal with his grief, as well as giving him a way to provide for me. It was his legacy, he always said." She did not want to think of what losing the claim would do to him. He would feel a failure, not just as a farmer but as a father.

"Come sit by me and say your prayers, child." Granny spoke gently, instead of in her usual acerbic tone. "Let the Lord carry your troubles for the rest of the night."

It was good advice, but Liza found that she was not able to stop worrying. The fire was getting low—a log sank down into a bed of glowing embers. She settled into the other rocking chair, wrapped a thick quilt around herself and stared into the embers.

Why had Matthew taken so long to come to her as he'd promised? She had waited, first hopefully, preparing the loft in the cabin for two people. Then anxiously, wondering if something had happened to him. She had no way of knowing where he had gone, exactly. Just a hastily scribbled note saying he was going to find gold and that he would come to her in the spring. Months had gone by, and not a word from him.

She was familiar with the feeling of being left. After Pa had headed off west, she had waited back in Iowa for three years before he had sent for her. Even though his concern had been to make sure there was a proper home for her, he had left her. That awkwardness still lay between them. They never spoke of it, but she could tell sometimes, when he was in one of his moods, that the guilt weighed on him. She still struggled with her anger at being left behind.

She had traveled the Oregon Trail with a respectable family that her pastor had introduced her to. They had been kind enough, though preoccupied with their own affairs. She hadn't realized how lonely she had felt until she met Matthew. He had been traveling without family, too, and somehow that had formed a bond that had quickly strengthened into something stronger. Or she thought it had. He'd asked her to marry him. He said he loved her. Had he changed?

The memory of those dark eyes, looking straight at her with no sign of recognition at all… She shivered, despite the quilts. One thought chased another through her mind until at last she fell back to reciting her favorite psalms to calm herself. Finally, she slept.

The next thing she noticed was sunlight falling warm on her face.

Granny bent over a kettle hanging by the fire. "Good morning. I just checked on your man. He's

still sleeping, but his color looks good. I'm thinking he's not hurt that badly. Looks like he's not been
eating regularly, worn himself down." She patted
Liza on the shoulder. "The tea is almost ready. I'll
be back later, see how you're getting on." She must
have read the apprehension on Liza's face, because
she added, "You'll be fine. The Lord knows what
He's doing."

It was quiet after Granny left. Liza stood in the
middle of the room. She could hear early-morning
noises outside: birds singing, the occasional rattle of
wheels as a wagon rolled by. From the back room,
nothing but silence. She had to face him. She was
dreading it. To put off the inevitable, she whipped
up a batch of biscuits. While they were baking, she
combed out her hair, braided it and pinned it up into
a crown around her head. Her mother had always
told her that her light blond hair was pretty, but Liza
found it annoying. It was too fine. Wisps slipped out
of the braid despite her best efforts.

Dallying over her hair was only putting off the
need to go in and talk to Matthew. She straightened
up and put her shoulders back. She had walked the
length of the Oregon Trail. She was not going to
fail at the end.

Despite her resolution, it took an effort to knock
on the door to the back room. When there was no
response, she opened the door tentatively. No sound
came from the blanket-covered mound on the bed.
She pushed the door open wider.

She laid down his folded clothes at the foot of

the bed, putting on top of the pile the comb and the newfangled harmonica that she'd found in his pockets. That was all he had had on him, no money or identification.

He didn't move, so she took a couple steps closer. She studied him as if seeing him for the first time. He'd always been thin, but now he was downright skinny. His cheekbones stood out prominently, and there were dark circles under his eyes.

Under the quilt, his legs twitched as if he were about to run. He looked so like a boy, with that strand of dark hair across his forehead. A troubled boy. Whatever he'd been doing, he'd not had an easy time of it.

Unexpectedly, tenderness welled up inside her. She smoothed the hair away from his face. Very lightly, she trailed her fingertips across his warm skin. She smiled.

His eyes flew open. Dark eyes, fierce as a hawk, stared straight into hers. Then he moved swiftly.

She found herself flat on her back on the floor, with those fierce eyes intent upon her and his hand at her throat.

He was back at Dutch Flat. Vince was still alive, making silly jokes, walking backward down the alley and smiling at him without a care in the world. Without seeing the three men coming up behind him.

He struggled to call out, to warn Vince to look behind him, but as in the way of dreams sometimes, he could make no sound. There was nothing he could

*do to stop it. It was all going to happen again, just
like it had before. He was too late.*

A hand touched his face. Lost in his dream, he
reacted instinctively.

Then he blinked, focused. He was looking
straight down into the clear gray eyes of a young
woman, a few inches away. She was a delicate little thing, skin like porcelain, wisps of golden hair
framing her face.

"Good morning," she said breathlessly. Even
though he still had his hand on her throat, she was
looking up at him as if she trusted him not to hurt
her. He didn't like it that she was looking at him
like that. He removed his hand, but he did not know
what to do next.

He was completely lost, no firm ground to stand
on. He did not know where he was. He realized that
he did not know *who* he was. He frowned down at
the young woman. "Do I know you?"

For a moment, he thought he saw an expression of
pain in her eyes. Then she blinked, and it was gone.
"Well, you used to. Could you let me up, please?"

He suddenly realized that their respective posi-
tions were not exactly proper. He sat up, backing
away from her until he reached the wall, and ran a
hand through his hair. His fingers found the bandage, and his frown deepened. His head throbbed.
So. He had been injured. Someone had bandaged
him and put him to bed. He looked at the woman.
"Who are you?"

She sat up, brushing herself off. She tried to

smile, but it looked stiff, awkward. She stopped. "Good morning," she started again. "I am Liza Fitzpatrick." She looked at him, clearly waiting for some kind of reaction.

"You will pardon me if I do not introduce myself." It was irritating to have to admit his ignorance. Gingerly, he got his feet under him and stood, extending a hand to help her up. "Are you hurt? Please accept my apologies, madam. I do not make a habit of accosting strange women first thing in the morning."

"Do you usually wait until the afternoon before you accost women?" She evidently regretted the flippant impulse as soon as she saw him turning red. In more contrite tones, she added, "I should be the one apologizing. I'm sorry I startled you. Shall we sit?" She dragged a barrel chair over to the bedside. He looked around for another chair. When he saw there was none, he sat on the very edge of the bed, muscles tensed.

Tentatively, she began, "You must be as uncomfortable as I am."

If that's the case, then you must be uncomfortable indeed. Not that it showed. The young woman—Liza—spread the skirt of her blue dress out as she sat, then she folded her hands in her lap. With her light blond hair framing her lovely face, she looked like the picture of a modest young lady, poised and neat. He felt unsure of everything about himself, and he hated it. Then he noticed that the tip of her shoe just showed at the edge of her skirt. She was tapping her foot, where she thought he could not see. The discovery made him feel a bit better. He wasn't the only one who was unsettled by this conversation.

"Your name is Matthew Dean."

Not even a twinge of familiarity at the name. "You have the advantage of me. How is it you know my name and I do not?"

"I know you. Or at least," she amended, "I used to. You came to see me last night. You were ill and fainted."

He wrinkled his brow. "I think I remember... something about that. It's rather vague. I hope I was polite."

"What *do* you remember?"

He started to shake his head, then stopped, his fingers going to the bandage at his forehead again. "Nothing. Nothing that makes sense, at any rate. It was dark. Men jumped me. I think... I think there might have been a woman there as well, but that hardly seems likely."

"What else?"

"There is nothing else!" He stopped. "I beg your pardon. This is extremely frustrating. It's as if—it's as if part of my mind is a locked room and I'm on the outside trying to break down the door. I don't know the first thing about myself."

"Well," Liza said, "I can help with that, at any rate. Yes, you do know me. You come from Illinois. We traveled out west in the same wagon train. We used to walk together. We started to talk and became friends. Then we became more than friends.

You asked me to marry you. Then you left me to go to California to look for gold."

A dry recital of words, sticking to the bare facts. He struggled to take it all in. "I recall none of those actions, madam."

Without any memories, he felt like half a man. He was engaged to this woman? It was hard to imagine. She was so close to him that if he reached out his hand he could touch that lovely face, run his fingertip down the curve of her cheek. His fingers longed to do just that. It was as if he knew her on some level that ran deeper than rational thought. But his mind kept listing objections as if he were arguing a case in court. "You mean I just showed up in your doorway last night after not seeing you for months? It seems wildly coincidental."

"Not if you were coming to see me." The tapping foot accelerated its tempo. "Honestly, you are acting like I am offering you a nice, fresh rattlesnake for breakfast. I am not making this up."

He didn't know what to think. Nothing felt real; he could find no solid ground underfoot. He was blundering about, a man out of his depth trying to find his way. He had no way of knowing if she was telling the truth. Some part of him kept insisting that beautiful women were not trustworthy. At the same time, an instinct deeper than all reason urged him to trust this one.

He spread out his hands in a gesture of apology. "Please don't misunderstand me. I do not mean to offend you. It's just—I can't begin to explain how unsettling it is not to remember such basic facts about oneself. Proposing marriage to a woman is the sort of thing that should stick in a man's memory." His smile was hesitant, but it seemed to put her at ease. The toe tapping stopped. She smiled back at him—not a polite, social smile but with the full force of her relief.

Matthew's smile faded. For a moment, it seemed the most natural thing in the world to take her in his arms. He had to stop himself from reaching out to her. This was hardly the sort of thought he should be entertaining in this situation. "Well." He cleared his throat, turned aside, pulled the folded clothes onto his lap. "I should get properly dressed."

She blushed and stood up. "I'll see to breakfast."

"Thank you." He could feel his own face heating up under the beard.

In the front room, Liza folded up the quilts and started setting the table for breakfast. She could cope so long as she had something to do.

She was aware of every sound of movement she heard from the next room. Her nerves were stretched taut, like fiddle strings keyed up for a concert.

As she was sweeping the floor, she saw a mouse scurry past, keeping close to the wall. She reacted instantly, whacking the broom down fiercely. She missed and whacked again. Peered down at the crack between the wall and the cupboard. "Where are you? You better get out of here if you know what's good for you."

"I think you made your feelings clear," came the dry voice from behind her. "He's probably halfway to St. Joe by now."

Matthew appeared in the doorway, dressed in his own clothes. He stood in the same position that he'd been in when he had walked through the front door last night, but one quick glance showed that he looked much better now. There was a healthy flush in his cheeks. He'd even introduced his hair to a comb, though it didn't look like they'd had much of a conversation. It was oddly endearing.

"The whole of the Oregon Territory is plagued with these varmints." She put the broom back in its place with a determined thump.

"It's still a large reaction for such a small nuisance."

She busied herself with putting food on the table. It was hard to meet his gaze directly. She needed to put some distance between the two of them, to come to terms with the reality of Matthew being back in her life. It was a relief to seize upon a neutral topic. "I can't abide mice. Over the winter, vermin like that got into my father's grain stores, ruined near half of it. I have no plans to buy wheat this winter." No funds to do so, either, but there was no reason to mention this. Matthew nodded, and somehow she had the feeling that he understood what she hadn't said out loud. She gestured at the table. "Sit. I've made biscuits, and there's some smoked salmon. Granny Whitlow said she would stop at Doc Graham's place, so the doc should be comin' by soon to make sure you're all right."

He did not sit down. Instead, his hands curled around the back of the chair and gripped. "I don't have any money."

"I have coin. I can pay him." *See? You need my help. You need me, even if it's only for a little while.*

"You've already given me a bed to sleep in. Now food and medical attention. And I've got no way to pay you back. I don't like accepting charity."

That stopped her. She set the crock of butter down with a thump and turned to face him, one hand on her hip. "One thing you're going to notice about life in this territory—people help each other. Especially when you've just arrived. The settlers who were already established helped my father when he came here, and they helped me, too, when I arrived. And now I'm helping you. We can talk about payment for the doctor later, if we must, but right now what you are going to do is eat." She pointed at the chair.

His eyebrows rose, but all he said was, "Yes, ma'am." He took his seat and unfolded the napkin she had provided. "It smells wonderful." He spread butter on one biscuit and added a spoonful of honey. Liza took one as well, but she only toyed with it, crumbling the edge. She had no interest in food. Though she kept her head down, focusing on her mug of tea, her attention was concentrated on the man sitting opposite.

He was trying to remember his table manners, clearly, but it was equally clear that it had been some time since he had eaten. He wolfed down the salmon and biscuits and eagerly accepted more. Finally, he put down his fork. "I hadn't realized how hungry I was. That was absolutely marvelous. Thank you."

"You're welcome." At least he appreciated her cooking, even if he appreciated nothing else about her.

He hesitated. "I have to say something, but I don't want to hurt your feelings. I've already thrown you to the floor and offended your notions of kindness. But it needs to be said. Even after that wonderful meal, and the tea."

"Granny Whitlow made the tea before she left. She insisted on staying the night, to keep people from gossiping." She wasn't sure why she offered that, except that she was fairly sure she did not want to hear whatever unpleasant topic he was going to bring up.

It worked to divert him. "Wait—you mean you were staying here all by yourself? How trusting are you? You need to be more careful in the future. Whatever happened to me last night, it seems clear there are dangerous people about. And for all you know, I could have been some kind of…unscrupulous man."

"You are the farthest thing from unscrupulous."

"I might have changed from the man you remember."

"People don't change," she said. "Not in essentials."

"*Far* too trusting. I am amazed that you've made it this far without being hurt. Staying all alone in a place. Smiling at a man. The world is not always a kind and safe place."

She was not going to budge him from his opinion of himself, that was plain. She got to her feet. "The McKays should be back today. I'll tidy up, and we'll be ready to go if the doc thinks you'll be up for it."

"Go? Go where?"

"Back to the claim." She had been reaching for his plate, but she stopped, straightening to look at him. "You can't stay here with the McKays. There's no room, with the children and all. You can stay on our claim while you rest up and figure out what to do next."

Taking a deep breath, he said, "I need to make something clear."

She wiped her hands on her apron and sat down. "That sounds very serious."

"I do not want to be in any way unkind, but I want you to understand my position. I appreciate you helping me out last night and giving me a place to sleep and a chance to get cleaned up. I am in your debt. But that doesn't mean I feel obliged to marry you."

The words fell like stones into the quiet room. He stretched his hands out across the table toward her in a plea for understanding. "To me, the man who asked you to marry him and the man who is right here in front of you are two different people. I am a stranger even to myself. I'm in no position to get married."

Her chin came up. "If you want to break off our engagement, that is your right."

"I cannot renege on an agreement I don't remember making."

"I suppose I can understand that."

Liza went back to clearing the table. She needed to do something with her hands. He was rejecting her all over again. And he sounded so reasonable about it, so calm. As if he had never really cared that much for her in the first place. The love that had once blazed between them stronger than anything she had known…not even an ember still flickered beneath the ashes.

Maybe he felt this way as a result of his injuries, but it still hurt.

A wall. She pictured building a wall, brick by brick, around her heart as a barricade. She just needed his help on the claim. No emotional entanglements. Strictly business.

"I—my father and I—need help to get the harvest in. If you would do that, then you could pay off your debt, as you call it. I don't think you owe me anything, but you'd be doing me a great favor if you did."

"I will consider it," he said slowly. "I am in your debt, without question. So long as you do not consider us engaged to marry."

There was that flick of pain again, like a little knife stabbing at her heart. "As if the man I promised to marry were a different person from yourself." No matter how much it hurt, she would not be weak.

She would use the pain to build another layer in the wall around her heart.

"From my perspective, he is."

Add another layer of bricks. "Except I told Granny Whitlow that you were my fiancé."

"I'll deal with the rest of the world later. Let's get things straight between the two of us first."

She wasn't sure exactly what that meant. She wasn't sure she wanted to ask, either.

Doc Graham arrived a little while later, his half-moon spectacles perched as usual at the tip of his nose, and his round face shining with perspiration, as if he'd been hurrying. Clearly, he had been primed with the latest gossip. His little blue eyes gleamed with curiosity as he escorted Matthew to the back room.

When the doctor came back out some minutes later, he smiled at Liza. "Don't look so worried. His injuries are quite superficial, apart from the cut on his head, and that should heal soon enough. Injuries can cause temporary amnesia—inability to remember. It's not that uncommon."

Matthew had followed him out of the back room, shrugging on his coat. "Will my memories come back?"

"The mind's a tricky thing. Memory could come back in dribs and drabs, or all at once. Given a bit of time, the injury should heal." He clapped Matthew on the shoulder cheerfully.

Matthew hunched his shoulders. "So, I could do manual labor?"

"Thinking of getting a job at the lumber mills in Portland, are you, until your memory comes back? I don't see any reason why not. Far as I can see, the fainting last night was caused by lack of food—for several days, judging by the state of you. Before this morning, when was the last time you ate?"

"I don't remember," Matthew said wryly.

"Ah. Yes. Of course. Well, regular meals, light work for the next day or so. You should be fine."

"Thank you, Doctor." Liza doled out some coins from her purse. She fought not to let her disappointment show. She had hoped the doctor could have given Matthew more help with regaining his memory. After she shut the door behind the doctor, she turned to face Matthew. "Have you made up your mind?"

"Yes." He looked grimly determined. "I will make a deal with you. You give me a place to stay while I try to get my memories back. Maybe you can help me to jolt my memory. In return, I'll work to get in your harvest. Do we have a bargain?"

He extended a hand. When she took it, he shook her hand with the brief, firm grip of a man sealing a business deal.

Time was, he would have kissed my hand.

"I accept," Liza said.

Chapter Two

The McKays were due to return to the dry goods store sometime around noon, but half the town decided to show up earlier. Or so it seemed to Matthew as, one after another, he met the townsfolk. Doc Graham was better than a telegraph operator for spreading news. Matthew's head ached trying to keep track of them all...

And if one more person made a remark about his engagement with Liza, he was going to lose all patience.

The dry goods store was far too small with this crowd pressing in on him. In reality, there were only a handful of well-intentioned townsfolk. But it *felt* like a crowd. Under normal circumstances, he would not have felt hemmed in, not had to fight down panic. It was the fundamental uncertainty of his life that made him feel so trapped. And these people kept asking him question after question.

He still had that feeling of having fallen into deep

water; he was in over his head and floundering. He desperately needed to find some solid ground to stand on. With no money and no memory, staying on the claim with Liza and her pa to help with the harvest was the only option that he could see. But these people were expecting more from him. They were going to be disappointed.

Pretty as Liza was, he couldn't imagine going through with an engagement in his current situation. He had no idea what had happened to him in the past year, since he and Liza had parted, and so he was in no position to make any long-term promises. For all he knew, he could already have a wife.

He was not the man she had fallen in love with. He'd accept her help as a business arrangement, so long as she understood that that was as far as their relationship went. They would help each other to achieve their goals. Nothing romantic in the least. He needed to make this clear from the start, so that everyone knew where matters stood.

A couple of women came up to him. He stood, offering his chair to the older of the two, Granny Whitlow. He wasn't sure whom she was grandmother to; it seemed more a title of respect rather than an indication of a familial relationship. The other woman introduced herself as Mrs. Graham, the doctor's wife. They had both been living in town for some years, apparently, so perhaps they could tell him things about Liza. What was she like, this woman who had attempted to claim him? If he had to live with her and her pa, it would help if he had some of idea of who she was, what kind of woman he was dealing with.

"Is it usual here for a woman to run a store all by herself?" He nodded toward Liza, who stood behind the counter helping a couple of children choose between the different sticks of candy.

"If that's the job that needs doing," Granny said. "Not too many women keep a store open as late as she did last night, though. Our Liza is the independent sort, likes to do things for herself—but of course you'd know all about that."

"Um…yes. Quite."

Granny gave him an odd look. "You two are supposed to be getting married, was my understanding. Seems to me you don't know much about the woman you're planning to spend your life with."

"On that subject—" Matthew began.

Mrs. Graham, the doctor's wife, intervened. "He's had a little problem with his memory, I understand." She smiled up at Matthew, her weathered face creased in kindly wrinkles. "Liza's been doing a fine job up here, helping her father on the claim and pitching in when other folk need things done, like minding the store for the McKays."

"Which she probably shouldn't be doing, not by herself." He wished he could remember something, anything, about the men who had jumped him the night before. It unnerved him, to think what might have happened if those men had followed him into the store.

A younger woman, wearing a purple bonnet with

feathers sticking out in all directions, came up to him. "I just heard you came all this way just to see Liza. You traveled up from California all by yourself?"

"Apparently," Matthew said.

"Now, Mavis Boone," Granny reproved her. "You keep batting your lashes at the man, he's going to think you're setting your cap for him. He's promised, mind."

Mavis blushed scarlet. "I was doing nothing of the sort," she said with some spirit. "I know full well he and Liza are getting married. She told me the story months ago. It just never seemed quite real. It always sounded more like a fairy tale, meeting a tall, handsome stranger on the trail." She shook her head. The foolish feathers on her bonnet bobbed up and down and in all directions. "And I hear that you're going to help Liza on the claim, too."

"Did Liza tell you that, too?" Granny asked her.

"No. Well, not exactly. She told Becky Weingard, and *she* told Hannah Shute, who mentioned it to Mrs. Taylor, who told me."

He wasn't even going to try to work that out. In a way, letting people continue to think he was engaged to Liza might protect him from flirtatious women. But it seemed this young woman was more interested in gossip. She wanted to know every detail of his life in California. He parried or evaded questions as best he could, but eventually he had to confess that there were gaps in his memory. That led to his recounting what he could remember about the men who had jumped him last night.

He hated having the story dragged out in the open. That was putting it mildly. Losing his memory made him feel like a helpless fool. Until his memories came back, he might as well be a prisoner or an invalid, a man with very little control over his life. Well, he had a say in his love life, at least. And he would not make any romantic commitments until he could remember his past.

All morning, Liza had kept an eye on Matthew as she dealt with customers. There were more people in the store than usual today. Many of them, having made their purchases, stopped by the rocking chairs near the fireplace to speak to Matthew. Several of the townspeople had already taken the opportunity to play a game or two of chess with him. As far as she could tell, he won all of his battles easily. She almost wished that he would lose occasionally; it would give him something to think about besides his troubles.

For he was brooding, she could tell. The tension in his shoulders and the way he set his jaw wouldn't have been noticeable to someone who didn't know him. He took the townspeople's scrutiny calmly enough. Occasionally a muscle twitched in his jaw, but he was polite to everyone who addressed him, even when Mavis Boone, who really should have known to behave better, flirted with him shamelessly, batting her eyelashes.

On the trail if something bothered him, he'd walked off his frustration. Here, she could see it building, with no way to vent. *Oh, Lord, it would really help if the McKays could come back early!* She could escape without having to introduce Matthew to Mr. Brown.

Then, as if on cue, Mr. Brown came through the front door. He doffed his hat, holding it before him. "Good morning, Miss Fitzpatrick. Might I have a word with you in private?"

"I can hardly leave all my customers." Liza indicated the group by the fireplace with a wave of her hand. They weren't actively shopping, but perhaps she could stretch a point and call them customers.

"I can wait," Mr. Brown said. Then he saw Matthew, standing between Mavis Boone and Mrs. Graham. His eyes widened, and he went very still.

"This is Mr. Dean," Liza said. "He's—" she started to say that he was her fiancé, but she stopped, remembering Matthew's request.

Granny Whitlow, however, had no reservations. "Mr. Dean here is her fee-an-say, come all the way from California."

The corner of Mr. Brown's mouth spasmed, as if he were holding back some strong emotion. "Indeed."

Matthew leaned back against the wall, folding his arms. He said nothing, merely raising one eyebrow. He returned Mr. Brown's stare with a steady gaze. "You seem familiar, somehow. Have we met before?"

Mr. Brown ignored the question. "I had heard that Miss Fitzpatrick's fiancé left her to go to California instead. I didn't get the impression that you'd been planning to come up here. Got tired of picking up all that gold?"

Matthew smiled, very slightly. "I am not sure why this is your concern," he said. He spoke in such a pleasantly neutral tone that Liza at first missed the sting underlying the words.

"Miss Fitzpatrick is my concern." Mr. Brown drew himself up to his full height. "I have a high regard for her, and her well-being is of the utmost concern to me." He turned to Liza. "I think perhaps you are right. This is not the right time for a private chat." He nodded toward the room. "Good day." Then he turned and headed for the door.

Mavis, never one to let go the chance to be the first to pass on gossip, added, "Mr. Dean was attacked last night. Right here in Oregon City!"

Mr. Brown paused and turned back to Matthew. "Indeed? How distressing. And have the miscreants been arrested then?"

Liza narrowed her eyes. There was an edge in Mr. Brown's tone. For some reason, this was not an idle question. He really wanted to know.

Mavis jumped in before Matthew could respond. "But that's just it, Mr. Brown. He's *lost his memory* as a result. It's like a story out of *Godey's* magazine! Just fancy!"

Mr. Brown smirked. "It does sound rather...fanciful."

"No doubt my memory will return in time," Matthew said smoothly.

Something flickered in the other man's pale green eyes, and his mouth pressed into a thin line. But he merely said to Liza, "I will speak to you another time."

When the door shut behind Mr. Brown, for a moment no one said anything. It was as if no one wanted to be the one to speak first. Predictably, Mavis broke the silence. She turned to Matthew with a smile. "Have you set a date for the wedding?"

Matthew heaved a sigh, as if pushed beyond all endurance. "I promised to stay for the harvest. Nothing more than that."

Mavis's mouth dropped to form an O.

"Oh, my!" Mrs. Graham said hurriedly. "I hadn't noticed that bolt of black trim that you have on the shelf. It must be new. What an unusual braided pattern. Will you show it to me, Liza dear?"

Liza fetched the bolt down from the shelf. She could feel her cheeks turning red, and she did not look in Matthew's direction once. The other townsfolk murmured one excuse or another and made their way out of the store. Mavis hurriedly decided that she wanted to look at the fabric with Mrs. Graham. Only Granny Whitlow remained next to Matthew, her eyes intent on his face, as if reading all the stress pent up inside him.

Matthew cleared his throat. "I, er, my headache seems to have returned. I think I'll go lie down in the back room until it's time to leave." He shut the door behind him.

There was an unpleasant moment of silence in the dry goods store. "Oh, my." Mavis Boone clicked her tongue.

"He's lost his memory," Liza said, a bit desperately. "It's completely understandable. He was attacked. He was hit on the head. He was—"

"He was quite definite," Mavis observed, her small eyes alight with eager malice. "Perhaps this isn't a fairy-tale romance after all."

Liza refused to allow her shoulders to slump. "He is ill," she said, with all the firmness she could muster. "It is unfair to judge him by anything he says while he is unwell."

"Of course," Granny said. "Mavis, Miz Graham, I think we have taken up enough of Liza's time today. I've got chores that need doing, and I'm sure you do, as well."

The door closed behind them, and Liza was alone. She immediately went and knocked on the door that led to the back room. At Matthew's muffled acknowledgment, she pushed the door open.

Matthew was sitting on the bed, looking down at his hands. He looked up at her as she turned to face him, putting her hands on her hips. "Could you please not do that again? It is humiliating to have you go around telling everyone that I mean nothing to you."

His eyebrows drew together. "That is not what I said. I wanted to make it clear that I am not planning to marry anyone when I can't even remember the first thing about myself."

"Yes, but there's no need to shout to the whole world that you want nothing to do with me."

"I told three people," Matthew snapped, his patience beginning to fray.

"You told Mavis Boone," Liza said grimly. "Trust me, everyone else in the territory will hear about it."

"I'm sorry if what I said hurt your feelings. That was not my intention."

She sighed. "I'm sure it wasn't." Her shoulders slumped, and she turned away and went back into the front room, shutting the door behind her.

When Matthew came out, Liza was making slow going of wrapping up the bolt of fabric that Mrs. Graham had been examining. She kept her eyes fixed on the fabric even when he came up to the counter. "I *am* sorry that I offended you," he said, his tone softer. "I thought I was being practical, making sure everyone knew that I was not in a position to continue an engagement made in the past. I should have thought of how it would sound. I didn't mean to hurt your feelings."

She returned the bolt of fabric to the shelf, but when she turned back, she still avoided his gaze. "I guess I understand how you feel," she said softly.

"Do you?" His tone was so low she barely caught it. "I wish I did. You have no idea how lost I feel right now." Then he turned and went back into the other room. The door shut behind him.

Liza closed her eyes for a moment, willing herself

not to cry. *Lord, please lead him out of his darkness. Lead him back to me. Or help me to let go of him for good.*

Chapter Three

The McKays arrived shortly before noon. After they paid her for her work, Liza and Matthew emerged into the bright sunshine of a fall day.

Matthew looked around in surprise. For some reason, he'd expected to see a rough wilderness settlement. Instead, he found himself on a street several blocks long, crowded with stores, homes and churches built from sawn lumber or even from brick. The sound of the waterfall upriver was a constant muted thunder.

Liza pointed down to where a barge was slowly ferrying a horse and wagon across the river. "That's how we get back to the claim, across the river and over the ridge."

Matthew blinked up at the sunlight. It didn't hurt him the way the lantern light had last night. He must be getting better. He turned to Liza. "Are we going there now?"

"Not yet. Come with me." She set off down the plank sidewalk.

He caught up with her easily, maneuvering around her so that he walked on the side by the dusty road. "Might I ask where we are going?"

"We're going to see Mr. Keller."

A pause. Drily, he asked, "And…should I recognize that name?"

"He's one of the people who came out on the wagon train with us. He runs the local newspaper now, so we'll be sure to find him in."

"What would meeting him achieve?"

"Seeing a familiar face might stimulate your memory."

"If seeing you didn't stimulate it, I doubt other people will be able to trigger it."

"Well, we won't know unless we try. Maybe they were more important to you."

He flicked a glance at her. Was there a note of resentment in there? She was stomping along on the plank sidewalk as though she had a personal grudge against it.

"Wait." She stopped in the middle of the sidewalk. Matthew took hold of her elbow and drew her aside to avoid a man coming the other way. She turned to face the opposite direction. "We should go see Frank first."

"Ah. Frank. Of course." Another pause. "Are you going to keep throwing names at me and expecting me to deduce who they are?"

She gave him a sidelong glance and looked away,

her cheeks a lovely shade of pink. "You never used to be this cantankerous. Frank Dawson is the local sheriff." She set off again.

"You are on a first-name basis with the sheriff? Is he a relative, by any chance?"

"For a man who doesn't plan to stay around, you surely ask a lot of questions. I'm trying to help you. If anyone can track down the men who attacked you, Frank can."

Possibly. And possibly he could find out what it was about the man that embarrassed her. He didn't like secrets. His whole life felt like a secret—one being kept from him.

Frank Dawson annoyed Matthew from the moment Matthew escorted Liza into the little office next to the jail.

His dislike had nothing to do with the overly familiar way the sheriff greeted Liza. Not his business. Well, unless she objected. Then he might get the opportunity to explain to the graceless lout that a gentleman did not put his paw on a lady's shoulder as if he had a right to touch her.

Sadly, Liza merely gave the oaf a polite nod and took a step back before seating herself on a chair next to the sheriff's desk. She looked expectantly at Matthew. He sighed, very softly, and sat down, as well.

The sheriff stared at him, tugging on his mustache, while Liza performed the introductions and explained what happened. Matthew got the impression that the sheriff didn't seem to think there was much he could discover, that a man should expect that kind of thing when you were this far from civilization. Still, he took down the details of the attack that Matthew could remember, such as they were. Then he laid down his pencil and turned to Matthew. "Fiancé, so I've heard. Fancy word for saying you're promised. Of course, people don't always keep promises." His chair creaked as the sheriff leaned back, steepling his fingers and studying Matthew.

Enough of this. Matthew was not a violent man, but the proprietary way this oaf was looking at Liza made his hands clench. He probably should leave before he said something ill advised. It was none of his business, so long as Liza didn't object. He had to remember that.

Matthew climbed to his feet. Liza rose as well, putting her hand on his sleeve. "We can't stay," she told the sheriff. "I just wanted to make sure you got all the details of the men who attacked Matthew."

The sheriff's mustache twitched as though he had more to say, but he just gave a short nod. Probably the man lacked the intellectual capability to carry out any sort of investigation, but Matthew wasn't sure what else to do. He was grasping at straws.

Their next stop was a humble clapboard building, painted white. It was wedged between two more pretentious buildings, whose false fronts made them look like proper two-story buildings until you saw behind the facade. "Are you busy, Mr. Keller?" Liza called.

"I'm always busy," a gruff voice responded from the back room before an older man with flyaway white hair emerged, wiping ink-stained hands on a rag. Matthew couldn't tell if Mr. Keller's face was flushed red from temper or exertion, but the man came up to the counter and nodded a polite enough greeting to them. "I never expected a newspaper to be a flourishing concern in such a small town, but every time an ox strays, whether accidentally or because some thief is leading it, people come racing over here demanding that I put a notice in the paper about it."

Matthew looked at Liza and shook his head. "I don't remember meeting this man before." Nothing about him sparked a memory. There were plenty of sparks when he looked at Liza, though not related to his memory. Safer not to think about that. The last thing he needed was a distraction, especially one with a lovely face framed by wispy blond hair.

"Maybe if he talks to you about things you said or did while part of the wagon train, that might spark a memory."

Liza explained his situation to Mr. Keller, and Matthew did his best to stand there and not feel like the latest exhibit in a menagerie. Mr. Keller squinted up at Matthew, started to say something, then stopped and squinted again.

The older man walked slowly around him like he was a horse being offered for sale. Matthew half expected the man to check his teeth. "Well—" His voice quavered. "Well, I don't know what to say. I remember your young man, but this don't look like him. I never talked to him all that much, anyway."

Well, then. That's that. Matthew started to take Liza's arm to escort her out, but she did not budge. Her eyes remained fixed on Mr. Keller. "You never talked with a man you saw every day for months?"

"He was pretty aloof on the trail."

"Quiet," Liza said.

"Kept to himself."

"Reserved." She crossed her arms and glared at Mr. Keller.

Matthew cocked one eyebrow at her. It felt odd, someone so dainty stepping up to be his champion. It was a new sensation, but he rather liked watching this little spitfire stand up for him. He said mildly, "The fact is that this man does not remember me and I do not remember him. We are back where we started."

Mr. Keller said, "I recollect that your man used to talk some with old Mrs. Martin, help her carrying water and such. Maybe you could ask her."

Matthew thought that Liza was forcing her smile as she thanked the other man. Certainly, this smile had nothing of the effect of the one she had given him when they were alone in the dry goods store. Thankfully.

He opened the door for her and followed her outside again. Standing on the plank sidewalk, he said,

"I'm not sure meeting people I'm supposed to know is having any effect on my memory."

"You can't be sure from just that one encounter. I'll introduce you to everyone we met on the wagon train if that's what it takes to help you remember." She sighed. "Except most of them aren't around this area. The available land near here was claimed before we came, so people went down south, toward Salem. Never mind. Meeting old Mrs. Martin will trigger your memory."

When they arrived at Mrs. Martin's place, her daughter-in-law listened to Liza's explanation, then she looked at Matthew doubtfully. "She's been feeling poorly of late. But I remember her telling us how kind the people she came out with had been. I was glad to hear it. It worried me that she came out on a wagon train without family to help her, but she said she had to come. After we left, she found she couldn't bear to be parted from Tad, not after losing her other sons."

She led them into a stuffy back room, smelling strongly of a mixture of lavender and licorice cough drops. An older woman sat in a rocking chair, reading her Bible. "Mama, this man here wants to know if you remember him."

He stepped into the room and stopped, assaulted by a memory. An older woman, the lines in her face carved from pain and years of hard work. Matthew frowned, trying to grasp the memory that had surfaced. Something about coming too late. Even as he reached for it, the image slipped away, elusive as a fish in a stream.

The frail older woman put down her book and took off her spectacles. She took one look at Matthew, and her face lit up with joy. "Yes, that's him! That's him. You've found him." Her hands came out to caress his cheek. Tears ran down her face. "That's him. That's my son Elliott." She asked Liza, "Have you seen his brother Quincy? They told me they got a fever and they died, but I knew better. I knew you'd come back to me."

Liza winced. This all was her fault. Matthew, looking intensely uncomfortable, tried to step back. Mrs. Martin clung to him, pressing her cheek against his jacket and crying.

"Madam, forgive me, but—" His voice faded. He raised one hand and gave a few tentative pats on her shoulder. "It will be all right." Liza had never heard him speak so gently. His deep voice carried conviction in a way that was subtly reassuring. "If the Lord took your sons, then He has them safe. He'll keep them in His heart until you can see them again. It will be all right." Despite his own obvious discomfort, he wanted to offer comfort to the poor woman.

Mrs. Martin's daughter-in-law roused herself from her mortified stupor and stepped in to soothe the older woman. Liza grabbed Matthew's arm and they left.

Out in the fresh air again, Matthew took a deep breath. His face was even more pale than it had been last night. "Please tell me there isn't anyone else you think I should meet today."

Something twisted inside her, right about the region of her heart, at the thought of putting him through any more trauma. "One more person. The barber. You were clean shaven when Mr. Keller and Mrs. Martin knew you. How can you expect anyone to recognize you when you look so different?"

"I do not currently possess any funds." He fingered the ends of his beard. "And you have already paid for the doctor's visit."

"I'll take it out of your wages," she said lightly. "You want people to recognize you, not run away in fright."

Under that fearsome beard, she thought that she saw one corner of his mouth twitch upward. "Lead on, m'lady."

While Matthew was at the barber's, Liza went to stock up on supplies. Coming down the sidewalk, she saw Mr. Brown walking toward her, his head bent so he did not see her. By his side walked Dr. Graham. They were deep in discussion. She hurried into Abernethy's mercantile store before they noticed her. Mr. Brown always made her uncomfortable. It was the way he stared at her. Made her feel as if she was touching a toad.

She bought tea, beans and, of course, salmon jerky, since it was so prevalent. If she could persuade her father to build a smokehouse, they could make their own. But that was a battle she would have to fight later. Once they harvested the grain, they'd have enough to live on through the winter. That was all she could concentrate on at the moment.

At least, that was all she could concentrate on before she stepped out of the store and saw Matthew coming down the sidewalk in his slow, easy stride.

She stopped moving. Somehow, she had forgotten how handsome he was. Clean shaven, with neatly trimmed hair, his impact swept over her like a physical wave. High cheekbones, elegant bone structure, those thin well-shaped lips that used to smile at her so easily. Only a bruise on one side of that square jaw and the thin red line by his temple reminded her of the injured man who had stood in her doorway last night demanding to know who he was.

He raised one eyebrow. "Do I pass muster?"

"I'm sorry?"

"You're staring."

She swallowed her disappointment. For a moment, she had expected him to be his old self again, holding out his hands to her and smiling. The new Matthew did not behave like that.

She felt sorrow for the loss, something precious as gold slipping through her fingers. If ever he loved her, that part of him was forgotten. Maybe he'd never loved her at all. How could she tell?

"You'll do." She hefted the basket with her shopping, but he slipped it from her grasp. He offered her his left arm, escorting her down Main Street for all the world as if he were promenading down the finest street in St. Louis on a Sunday afternoon. Despite her depression, she spared a moment to be amused by his air. He had always treated her like a rare precious object. Right up to the point he had left. How many other women had he treated in the exact same manner while he'd been away? Granny Whitlow's comment about all the pretty women in California was probably true. She sighed. He looked at her sideways but made no comment on her mood.

When they got to the livery stables, they found Frank Dawson leaning against the wall, arms folded. He ignored Matthew and spoke to Liza. "I'd like a word with you."

Matthew frowned, but he handed the basket back to her. "I'll help harness the horse."

Frank waited until Matthew was out of earshot before he spoke. "Are you serious about that man? He looks like a vagabond, from what I can tell."

"I thought he looked much more respectable now that he's had a shave and a haircut."

"He doesn't seem like the man you described when you came up here, is all."

"Frank Dawson, I told you I was engaged the first time I met you." Her hands gripped the basket more tightly, and she narrowed her eyes at him. "Are you thinkin' I'm a liar?"

He held up his hands. "Whoa! Don't be so hasty. I'm thinkin' you don't know what you want. And this man just dropped in out of nowhere. You might be mistaken."

"I'm not."

"You just watch yourself, that's all. Don't trust him too far. I'll let you know if I hear anything."

She nodded, but she did not relax until he was out of sight. Frank wasn't a bad person, and she liked him, but she wished he wasn't so protective. She wasn't the least bit interested in him romantically. She had been clear on that point from the day they met, but he wasn't listening. None of the men in her life seemed to want to listen to her. She wanted what she had had with Matthew on the trail—that sureness of belonging with him—wanted it so badly that she ached with the loss. The loss felt like missing a part of herself. If he no longer wanted her, well, she would have to accept that. But she would not settle for less. She knew the difference now.

As she climbed into the wagon, Matthew dropped something small into her lap. "Here."

She looked down. A black-and-white bundle of fluff was making a determined effort to climb up her bodice. Round green eyes met hers, innocent and curious. "What is this?"

He very deliberately did not look at her. Instead, he settled into the seat next to her, took up the reins and flicked them against the horse's rump. As the horse started to move off, she was distracted from the little bundle of energy in her lap to protest. "I can drive."

"The fact that you are able to do so does not in any way imply that you should *have* to do so."

"You can't expect me to sit here like a fine lady from back east who does nothing." She couldn't decide whether to laugh or to scowl right back at the man. "It is a bit late now for me to start acting all

helpless. Since you left, I've learned to fend for myself. I had to. And you are avoiding the subject of
this cat."

"Kitten," he said, still looking ahead instead.
"Only a couple months old. I have it on good author-
ity that he likes having his ears 'scritched.' Turns
out Jim Barnes felt the need for a harmonica. I suggested a trade."

"You thought I needed a kitten?"

"He can catch mice for you."

She looked doubtfully down at the little kitten,
still trying to climb her dress, and then back up at
Matthew.

"Eventually," he amended. His tone was noncha-
lant, and he kept his eyes fixed on the road ahead,
but she could see his ears were turning a bit red.

She scratched the kitten under the chin and then
moved up to behind the ears. The little animal closed
his eyes and purred loudly. She had to smile. "Thank
you."

Once across the river, they rode in silence as the
trail wound its way through a forest of big-leaf maples and bitter cottonwood trees. Occasionally they
would pass a clearing with a log cabin surrounded
by fields of buckwheat or corn or rye. Most of the
settlers in this area were already at work harvesting their crops, the men scything the grain while
the women bundled the sheaves into shocks to dry.
Children ran to and fro carrying water to the adults
sweating in the hot sun.

After a few miles, the road narrowed to nothing

more than a deeply rutted trail beside a creek that wound its way into the thickly forested hills. Trees arched overhead, and encroaching branches reached out on either side. She had to duck under one that tried to snag her bonnet.

She was extremely conscious of every breath taken by the silent man next to her. They were forced to sit so close together on the bench that his coat sleeve brushed against her shawl. Thankfully, keeping ahold of the restless kitten gave her something to do with her hands.

They had never simply sat like this before, just the two of them alone. When they sat together, it had been with the others around the campfire. On the trail, they had walked side by side through the grasslands and the badlands, talking about what their future would be like in Oregon. They were going to have six children. She'd picked out their names. He had laughed and said he'd better keep practicing law as well as working the land. It had seemed so simple back then. Anything was possible; everything she'd dreamed of was within reach.

When they had fallen in love, she had thought they would spend the rest of their lives together. But Mavis had been right; that had been a fairy-tale romance. Now it was daylight.

All this past year, she had nursed a secret hope that Matthew would come back to her. Even as he stayed away and stayed away, and no word came, she'd kept the dream alive by picturing him returning, coming in the door and sweeping her off her feet and solving all her problems. Mr. Brown would cower before him, her father would cheer up—everything would be wonderful.

Reality was like cold water thrown in her face.

He handled the horse competently, with minimum fuss, until the road forked. One track continued on straight, while the other turned left over a bridge that crossed the stream. He stopped the wagon. "Is it really so difficult to provide signposts? Which way?"

Wry amusement lightened her mood a trifle. The man needed to be taught a lesson in the perils of being overprotective. "Folks round here know where they are and where they want to be. If you don't know where you're going, then it makes no sense for you to be doing the driving."

His thick eyebrows drew together, a crease forming between them. "Which way?"

She leaned forward to rescue the kitten, who was batting at the loose reins as they dangled from Matthew's fingers. Then she sat back. "I never thought to ask about your ancestry," she said sweetly. "I'm guessing half man, half mule."

He heaved a sigh, then dropped the reins and gently gathered up the kitten out of her hands. "Fine. You drive, I'll scritch."

She picked up the reins and clucked to the horse, who moved forward across the bridge. The wheels rolling across the half logs created a hollow sound, like the rumble of distant thunder. "You're awfully stubborn about taking charge of things, considering you aren't planning on staying long." She couldn't let it go; she had to keep picking at the topic like a scab over a wound that wouldn't heal.

He gave her a sidelong look. "I do not mean to imply that you are not able to drive. But women should not have to fend for themselves."

"Maybe more than half mule."

"Surely you acquainted yourself with my defects before agreeing to marry?"

She tried to make her voice sound light and indifferent. "I must have been blinded by love."

"How romantic." From his tone, nothing could be more unappealing. He buttoned the kitten into his jacket. She could hear a contented purring start up inside. At least one of them was happy.

The trail began to wind up a low ridge. Fir trees began to replace the maples and cottonwoods. Liza pointed out the ridge on the west. "On the other side of that ridge is the Baron's land. He hauls his logs down to the river and sends them to his lumber mills in Portland. If he bought the claim from Pa, he'd have a faster route to the river. That's why Mr. Brown keeps pestering us about selling the claim."

Matthew frowned. "How is Mr. Brown involved?"

"He works for the Baron." Liza shrugged. "He wants to keep his boss happy."

"The way he looks at you, that's nothing to do with business," Matthew said darkly.

They came over the brow of the hill and began the gradual descent to her own little valley. She could feel the tension ease out of her muscles like an invisible tide receding, leaving peace in its wake. She was home.

They had arrived at the most beautiful time of the day. The late afternoon sun filtered through the trees, its slanted rays turning the grain in the fields to a sea of gold. The wheat was just ripe enough to harvest. In the pasture, the few cows they possessed cropped the grass peacefully, while chickens scratched outside the newly constructed barn.

It gave her a warm feeling every time she came home and caught sight of the cabin through the trees. One day, they'd have money to put glass in the windows instead of oiled paper. The setting sun would reflect light off the windows. She could picture it, the cabin turning into a gracious home, the grasslands becoming cultivated fields, the vast potential that lay untapped in this beautiful land being realized.

This was where she had planned to put down roots, raise a family. *Oh, Lord, please let him love this place as I do.* Even if he were leaving, she wanted that. Then it would be as if he loved her still, just a little.

Putting off this moment was not going to make it any easier to say what she had to tell him. He had been very clear that he was going to leave At least this time, he was honest about not staying. Well, then, she would be equally plainspoken with him. She had grown stronger in this year without him. If he did not want to be with her, she would survive. She would not let him break her heart again.

She stopped the wagon. The horse shook its head and let out its breath in a sigh, no doubt impatient at being stopped so close to its home. Then it stretched out its neck and began to nibble on the grass at the verge of the track. Liza turned to face Matthew. "This is my home."

"Yes." A light breeze lifted his dark hair out of his wary eyes.

"I need your help with the harvest. After that, consider your debt paid." She took a deep breath. "But if you leave this time, don't expect me to wait for you to come back." Her heart broke, just a little, at the words. But they needed to be said. She could not go through the pain of being left yet again. She had to protect herself.

The silence between them seemed to stretch into eternity. Not even a breath of wind to rustle the leaves in the maple tree by the track. Only the sounds of the horse cropping the grass and the faint purr of the kitten inside his coat. He did not move. She wanted to sink down into the long grass by the side of the trail and hide there. She could not bear it. He wanted nothing to do with her.

Finally, he spoke. "In your position… I would probably do the same thing."

Apparently, that was all he had to say on the matter. She picked up the reins and clucked to the horse to finish their journey. His response did not make her feel any better. It only reinforced her growing suspicion that the man she had fallen in love with on the Oregon Trail was truly gone. Matthew no longer loved her.

And she was still as much in love with him as ever.

Chapter Four

As the wagon began its slow, rattling descent into the valley, Matthew brooded over the injustice of his situation. Liza blamed him for abandoning her on the trail. Not only did he have no explanation for leaving her, he could not even remember doing so. If that wasn't bad enough, he had to spend several weeks living on this claim, and he had no idea how to deal with her. He could only fall back on his instinct that women needed to be protected. At least she understood that he didn't plan to stay around and marry her.

His thoughts spun round and round until he almost felt dizzy. He was going to get a headache again if he didn't relax. He took a deep breath, then let it out slowly. He just had to fulfill his bargain with Liza, and then he would be on his way again. He still felt guilty about the situation. There was no way to avoid feeling like a cad.

Liza started to speak, then stopped. Tentatively,

as if picking her way through a field of boulders, she said, "I should explain something. My father is not well. A tree fell the wrong way and landed on his legs. Broke them, one in two places. They're healing—he's able to get around the house and walk a little—but it's hard for him. A woman from the Kanaka mission came by to help him with daily chores while I was in town." They had reached the valley floor. The track led up to a small rise on the far side of the narrow valley, to a log cabin. She went on, "He might be...he gets a little cantankerous at times. It frustrates him that he can't get around and do everything he wants. I thought I should mention that he might be in a bad mood."

Wonderful. This day just keeps getting better and better.

The cabin was typical of the dwellings that Matthew had seen on their way here, small but sturdy, built of whole logs with a roof that projected out a few feet to provide a protected porch. Only a thin wisp of smoke rose from the chimney, and no candlelight showed through the oiled paper in the window. As the wagon rolled to a stop in front of the cabin, the whole setting looked idyllic.

At least, it did until they heard the singing.

"What on earth is causing that caterwauling?" Matthew demanded. "Is someone torturing a cat in there?" From inside his coat, the kitten popped its head out, ears pricked inquisitively. He stroked it between the ears and it started to purr again, the peaceful sound a stark contrast to the dreadful tuneless sounds coming from inside. He started to get out so he could offer a hand to Liza as she descended, but she scrambled down without waiting for him. She had her shoulders hunched, as if to ward off what waited for her inside.

Liza pulled the string on the door, lifting the latch inside, and pushed the cabin door open wide. After the bright sunshine, the cabin seemed very dark. Looking over her shoulder, Matthew could make out a table, a couple of benches, one on its side, and a cat-and-clay fireplace with only embers glowing. He could just discern a man sitting at the table, slumped forward, his head bent. A half-finished loaf of bread, a hunk of cheese and two plates were on the table… as well as an empty jar, lying on its side. He could not see much more than that. But he did not need sight, not when his sense of smell could tell him all he needed to know. His nose wrinkled.

"Oh, no." Liza went to the man at the table, who was still crooning softly. She set the empty jar upright. "Pa, you said you weren't going to buy any more. You promised faithfully." Her voice broke on the last word, and without thinking Matthew stretched out a hand to her. She did not notice, focused as she was on her father. He let his arm drop and clenched his hand into a fist. There was nothing he could do to help ease her distress.

The man mumbled something, his words slurring together so that Matthew could not make out what he was saying. Then the man repeated himself, louder. "Didn' buy anything. Gift, thas what it was. Being neighborly. Thas all. The man kindly shared his drink. Social."

"Was it Mr. Brown? He didn't ask you to sign anything, did he?" Even in the dim light of the cabin, Matthew could see Liza's face had turned white.

"No, no." He mumbled the words, his eyes closing as he angled his head back against the pillow. "I didn' sign anything. I kept my promise. I'm not like that man of yours." Her father's eyes closed, and he sighed deeply. "It was just a verbal agreement. 'A gentleman's agreement,' he said." Her father's mumbling faded away into snores. His mouth relaxed, and he rolled his head over until it was pillowed on one arm.

Liza shook him by the shoulder. "What was the agreement? *Pa, what did you agree to do?*" But her father's snores rolled on, unimpeded.

She looked around at the cabin and shook her head helplessly. "I don't even know where to begin." She focused on Matthew again. "This isn't like him, not usually. Pa hasn't had anything to drink in, oh, in months. Truly."

It seemed important to her that he understood that, so he nodded. "Where does he sleep?"

"He sleeps in the back room. I sleep up in the loft." She bit her lip. "I could put a blanket down on the floor in the back room for you?"

"Let's worry about that later. First things first."

She leaned forward to pick up a plate. Then she put it back down again. She sighed. "The cows need milking, and I need to check on the chickens, take care of the horse, get my father to bed, clean up the house…"

He felt an odd impulse to reach out, take her in his arms and comfort her. That was impossible, of course, so he scowled. "I'll get your father to bed and then tend to the horse."

"Do you feel up to it? You're not dizzy or anything?" She looked up at him, those clear gray eyes showing her gratitude. Warmth swept through him when she looked at him like that. It was distracting. His scowl deepened, and she looked away, her face turning red.

"If I start to feel faint, I'll rest. You go tend to the cows and feed the chickens." He couldn't help it. He gave in to his need to touch her. Sliding a finger under her chin, he lifted her face up until she met his eyes. "It'll be all right. You'll see." He dropped his hand hastily and took a step back.

He got Liza's father into bed with some difficulty. Though the older man was not tall, he was broadly built and heavily muscled. He leaned heavily against Matthew as he stumbled across the back room to the bed. Matthew eased the other man down onto the bed. Still only half-conscious, the older man sighed deeply. "Don't be angry, Katy girl. I'll make it up to her."

Matthew removed the man's boots and drew a quilt over him. Heading outside, he unharnessed the horse and rubbed it down before setting it loose in its paddock. Then he went back to the cabin and built up the fire until it had begun to light the room with a cheery red glow. The kitten seemed content to crouch under a bench and watch him. He was just looking around for a candle to light when Liza came in. A wooden yoke was slung across her shoulders, and a pail of milk hung down from a rope on either side.

"It'll be a simple meal tonight. I brought bread and cheese from town, some apples, smoked salmon."

"That sounds lovely," he said politely. His stomach was so hollow, it was starting to make growling noises. Hopefully, she couldn't hear it. He found the stub of a candle set in a saucer and lit it. Light spread throughout the room.

"He took out the chess set." Liza squatted down to pick up the chess pieces, which had spilled out over the puncheon floor.

Matthew knelt down to help her, picking up pieces and putting them into their little box. He fingered one of the pawns, rubbing the polished wood with his thumb.

She glanced over at him. "Does it look familiar? You left it with me when you took off on the California Trail instead of coming with us out to Oregon."

He stared down at the piece. "Yes, I…no." He put the piece in the box. "I thought there was something, but it's gone."

"It will come back. You just need patience."

"Not my most noted quality," he said darkly.

She gave him a half smile. "Looks like we have something in common after all."

His eyebrows flicked upward. Was she flirting with him? No, apparently not. She had gone back to picking up the chess pieces, her head bent and her eyes on the floor. "I taught Pa how to play a little. He indulges me, but it's not his favorite way to pass the time. He'd far rather tell stories." She frowned. "The Baron loves chess. So does his assistant, Mr. Brown. He used to come by and challenge me to a game. He said I was a very good player."

"He didn't strike me as an especially honest man. Possibly he was trying to sweeten you up. A man tends to compliment a beautiful woman rather than criticize her."

After supper, Liza was tired, but far too restless to sleep. On impulse, she asked Matthew to come outside. There was a question she needed to ask, even though he most likely could not answer, and she did not want to chance her father overhearing her.

The sun had disappeared behind the western ridge. In the east, the last rays of the setting sun still lit up the white snow at the very tip of Mount Hood, but on the claim it was growing dark. All the better. She had a feeling this conversation would be easier if she couldn't see Matthew. If he were feeling sorry for her, she had no desire to see the pity on his face.

She sat down on the bench outside the cabin and motioned for him to join her. Matthew seemed hesitant, careful to leave some space between them when he sat down, and he looked around the claim rather than at her. Even so, she was extremely conscious of him, the mere physical presence of the man.

He had rolled up his sleeves to help her clean up the cabin; she could see the wiry black hair that lightly furred his forearms. His hands were strong, the fingers long and graceful, but terribly battered. Even in the fading light, she could see the scar that ran across the back of his left hand along the knuckles. That was new, but his hands were still achingly familiar to her. Hands that had once held hers as they had walked, hands that had brushed her hair back from her face as he looked down and smiled at her. She swallowed. Letting go of the past was harder than she had expected. Maybe it would be easier if she could at least get this one mystery cleared up.

She sneaked a glance at him out of the corner of her eye. He had tilted his head back to watch the sunset tint the white snow on Mount Hood to a warm apricot. The eastern sky beyond was darkening to a lovely royal blue. He seemed absorbed in admiring the scenery. Or pretending he was somewhere else. She wasn't sure how to work up to her question, but she had to start somewhere. "How are you feeling?"

He glanced at her briefly before returning to his appreciation of the sunset. "I am feeling quite well. The doctor seems to have made an accurate assessment of my injury being slight. I do not think you need to worry about my helping with the harvesting."

"I'm glad to hear it. I apologize for my pa. He really doesn't drink any longer. I'm sure he wouldn't have indulged if his visitor hadn't insisted."

"Do you still think it was this Baron?"

"Or Mr. Brown." She considered. "On the whole, I'd say he's worse than the Baron. At least the Baron comes at you straight on. Mr. Brown likes to sneak around and spring things on you when you least expect it."

She had Matthew's attention now. He was looking at her intently. "Has this Mr. Brown been pestering you?"

Now it was Liza's turn to admire the sunset. The snow on the mountainside was fading from apricot into a cool lavender. "I s'pose you could call it that. He used to like to come by and visit. I thought he was coming by to see Pa, at the time. He would chat with Pa for hours and then he tried to act all friendly with me. He said he was just being social."

"Men often expect women to appreciate their attentions."

"He does, at any rate."

He was still looking at her, she could feel it. "If he pesters you again…well, maybe he'll stop doing that if he sees that I'm staying here."

"Maybe. That's a problem I'll deal with when it comes, if it comes. I wanted to ask you about something else. I was wondering…there's one thing I'd really like to know. Why did you leave me?"

He sat unmoving in the half darkness, just watching her. "Why did I…?"

"If you ever get your memory back, I'd take it kindly if you would answer that question for me." She hugged her elbows to herself. Being left—

again—didn't get any easier. There was a hole in her, an aching absence that had once been filled with someone she loved and who loved her back.

He bent his head, looking down at his empty hands as though he expected them to hold answers. "I'm sorry. I'm afraid I do not understand. Are you telling me that your fiancé left without a word of explanation?"

"You left a note." She shifted uncomfortably. The bench could be improved with a cushion or two; it seemed harder than rock. "But all the note said was that you were heading off to find gold in California. And that you'd come looking for me in Oregon City."

Quietly, he said, "And now you want me to explain why I left? And didn't come back? Those are fair questions, but they're not for me to answer. I thought we had agreed that I am not that man. Not at the moment."

"It's just that—you left without saying goodbye. I—I keep wondering why. You could have come to see me before you left. If you've promised to marry someone, that seems like the least kindness you could do."

The ache inside her deepened. She had never spoken about this to anyone. It was easier to talk about it in the semidarkness when she could not see his face, note his expression. Somehow, sitting with him in the near dark, with the smell of the wood smoke from the chimney and the feel of tired muscles after a long day brought back the sensations that she associated with their days on the trail and the easy, comfortable familiarity between them. Back then, there wasn't anything they couldn't talk about.

"I am sorry that I cannot help you." His deep voice had gentled to a regretful murmur. "Perhaps if I can do something to trigger my memory's return. I recognized the chess set, or half recognized it. It looks familiar, but I cannot recall anything specific in regard to it. I do not recall playing chess, or teaching anyone else to play it, either."

"I can tell you things about yourself, if that would help." She doubted that would cause his memory to suddenly reappear, but what could it hurt? It would be something, at least. This ache inside her was just getting larger the more time she spent in the company of this stranger who had once said he loved her. So she started to tell him about himself, growing up in Illinois, getting the chance to study law at some fancy college in Boston before coming back to his hometown to settle down. There were some areas of his life that he hadn't said much about. He'd taken a trip to Europe but hadn't gone into much detail about what he'd seen there. He rarely spoke of his father, who had died while Matthew was quite young. She had gotten the impression of a stern older man who discouraged affection.

As she spoke, the snow up on the peak of Mount Hood faded from pale lavender to gray. Stars started to come out overhead. The claim lay cradled by hills, so she couldn't see the wide sweep of stars that she had seen on the prairie at night, but it was a comfort to still recognize the same familiar constellations they had looked up at together in the evenings on the trail.

Matthew listened intently, making few comments. It was odd to be the one doing all the talking. She had loved to sit by the campfire on the trail and listen to him rolling out tales of life back east, or of stories he had read. It didn't matter what he said—she had loved the sound of his deep, melodious voice.

Of course, in those days, she would have been sitting right next to him, feeling the warmth of his arm resting beside her, feeling safe and loved.

Loneliness speared through her, so sharp the pain was almost physical. The space between them was a few inches and an immeasurable gulf at the same time. She was alone in a relationship meant for two. It wasn't enough for him to be there physically if what they had between them was no longer there. She had to keep reminding herself that things were different now. Sitting here next to him hadn't been such a good idea. It would be so easy to give in to the illusion that he still loved her—if indeed he ever had.

She needed to focus on what she had brought him out here for. Stopping in the middle of a description of his childhood in Illinois, she said abruptly, "Let me ask the question another way. If you were to leave a woman, what would strike you as a good reason?"

She could hear the scuff of his boots on the ground as he shifted around to look toward her. She had no idea what he could see. He was a dim figure, his features lost in shadow.

"I cannot think of any good reason to leave a woman. Not if I loved her," he said.

Well, that was clear enough. She got to her feet. She was not going to cry in front of him—she would *not*. She turned away. "It's late, and we need to get an early start tomorrow. I should get you a blanket."

Matthew rose from the bench slowly, startled by Liza's abrupt departure. He had been taken off guard by her question and given an honest answer. Clearly, that had been a bad idea. He hadn't meant to hurt her. But she had to understand that whatever had gone on between her and her fiancé, it was nothing to do with him. His reasoning seemed logical. All the same, he had to fight down a feeling of guilt.

When he went back inside the cabin, Liza was climbing down from the loft with an enormous quilt slung over her back. She thrust it at him, avoiding his eyes. "Here. You'll want this. It's a thick, heavy quilt. I've spread out a blanket and pillow by the fire, but you might get cold."

He took the quilt. He had never stopped to look at quilts before, never considered them one way or another, but this one had a beautiful design on it, dark greens and blues and reds in an intricate pattern of interlocking geometric shapes. It was made of a tightly woven fabric that would keep out drafts.

He wanted to thank her, but she took a step back

and would not meet his eyes. "Well, I'll say good-night then."

His blanket was lying close enough to the fire that it felt comfortably warm as he lay down. The quilt was a snug barrier against the evening chill. He was well fed and tired enough so that sleep should have come easily. But as he lay there staring up at the ceiling, all he could think about was the look on Liza's face as she turned away from him.

He must have hurt her worse than he thought. He would have to find a way to make it up to her later. She was a good woman, even if she kept expecting things from him that he could not give her. Or perhaps she was having second thoughts about having him stay. He wasn't going to be here very long, after all. Then she and her father could get back to living their lives any way they liked. Without him. That thought was oddly disturbing, but before he could analyze why, he fell asleep.

A dark-haired woman, half-hidden in shadows of a side alley. She stretched out her hand, calling for his help. He went toward her. You were supposed to help women in distress. Something about her behavior seemed odd, forced. Then he heard footsteps behind him and harsh voices.

Pain. Someone hit him. The woman turned away. Fighting back, swinging blindly. More than one man was attacking him. He was surrounded. Trapped. A fist connected with the side of his head, and he stumbled into the wall of the alley. He bit his lip. He tasted blood in his mouth. More blood dripped into his eyes, blinding him. He struck out wildly and felt his fists connect with flesh. A grunt of pain from someone else. He was falling. With a cold shock, black water closed over his head. He could not tell which way was up. He panicked, flailing his arms and legs around in all directions.

He woke with the old, familiar feeling of hostile eyes watching him. With his eyes still closed, he slipped his hand under the pillow for the knife. But there was no knife there. Then he remembered. He had been attacked. Everything was gone, including his memories. But someone was there, standing to the side of the quilt. He could hear the heavy, labored breathing. He lifted his eyelashes a fraction. A big figure, standing there watching him. Matthew tensed his muscles, prepared to move quickly.

"Ah, looks like you are starting to wake up." A man's deep, gravelly voice. "Or are you going to lie there pretending you're still asleep?"

Chapter Five

"Pa? What are you doing?" Liza's voice, curious and unafraid.

Matthew opened his eyes slowly. A thickset man with sparse white hair was looming over him, but he wasn't paying attention to Matthew. His head was turned away. Matthew followed the direction of his gaze and saw Liza descending the last step of the ladder. He sat up quickly, ambushed again but a lot less able to defend himself. She had evidently been in the middle of getting dressed: she wore a pink calico dress, and her light hair cascaded down her shoulders, flowing down over her body like a field of newly ripened grain rippling in a breeze.

The sight was mesmerizing; he had to make an effort to look away. He had better find something else to focus on, and quickly. Liza's father was glaring at him again. Then for some reason the man shifted his gaze down to the quilt and then back to

Matthew. This time the look in those blue eyes was positively murderous.

Seemingly unmindful that her hair was flowing loose around her, Liza wrapped a shawl around herself, looking from one man to another. "I guess maybe I should introduce you. Pa, this is Matthew Dean. You remember that I mentioned him? We... we met on the trail. Now he's come over to help us with the harvest." In a few brief words, she described Matthew's attack and his resultant loss of memory. "The doctor thinks it's only temporary, though. He'll stay on the claim and get his memory back while helping get in the harvest."

Mr. Fitzpatrick did not look appeased. If anything, his bad mood had intensified. He glowered like a grizzly disturbed in its den.

Matthew got to his feet. None of the usual formulas used in this sort of situation seemed to fit. "Pleased to meet you" was not really appropriate, considering he had—technically—met the man the day before. Besides, he wasn't sure he *was* pleased to meet him. He didn't know what Liza had told her father about him, but it must have been something fairly unpleasant, judging by the way his mouth had tightened into a thin line.

People kept blaming him for actions he could not remember taking, promises made by another man inhabiting the same body. He settled on acknowledging her father with a nod. Didn't seem to help.

Liza looked from one to the other. She said,

brightly, "Pa, why don't you get dressed while I get breakfast ready?"

Mr. Fitzpatrick did not glare at Liza, Matthew noted. He grabbed a couple of thick branches that were leaning against the table, and Matthew realized that they were a pair of crudely carved crutches. Hunching over them made Liza's father seem smaller, but no less menacing. He thumped the crutches down as he made his way to the back room, grunting a little from the effort.

Once the door had slammed behind him, Liza looked at Matthew. "Good morning."

"Good morning." He looked at her and then quickly looked away. Didn't the woman realize that she was alone, her hair down, with a man she wasn't married to?

She seemed perfectly at ease, deftly braiding her hair into a plait and securing it with a strip of leather. He wasn't sure if this were excessive trust or a mere lack of understanding of men. Perhaps a mixture of both. "I'll go milk the cows, get us some milk for breakfast. There are always eggs, and I can whip up some biscuits."

He nodded. "Right. What do you want me to do?"

"If you could go fetch water? The bucket's over there. Pa's too proud to admit it, but it's not easy for him to get around, and managing the bucket and the crutches both is a hardship."

"Of course." And maybe he could splash a little cold water on himself, as well. Erase from his memory the picture of her with her hair falling loose around her. The last thing he needed was a distraction like that, especially under the critical eye of her pa. Protective of his child, and not inclined to welcome any stranger. Probably even if Matthew had ridden up on a white horse after slaying a dragon, Mr. Fitzpatrick would have been suspicious and prickly. A man who had to be told his own name was not going to inspire confidence.

When he opened the door, the little kitten slipped between his legs and set out to explore, but Matthew stopped dead in his tracks.

The cabin faced east, and so he was confronted with the full impact of the immense, snow-covered Mount Hood. In last night's dusk, he hadn't noticed how the massive volcano dominated the eastern skyline. Below lay ridge upon ridge of dense forests, nature unmarred by any sign of humanity.

This was the rustic wilderness he'd been subconsciously expecting. He could have been twenty miles from civilization or two hundred. Not even the smoke from a neighbor's chimney to remind him of the world outside. Everything he depended on for his daily survival was right here, in this little valley with these two people.

No wonder Liza had fired up and lectured him about relying on your neighbors. This was not a territory where you could survive without help.

To the north, farther off, a thin wisp of smoke around the summit marred the near-perfect symmetry of Mount Saint Helens. The thought of living in a valley with volcanoes on the horizon was beautiful and intimidating and strange, all at once. That seemed more to belong to Naples, and the teeming, overpopulated chaos around Mount Vesuvius.

He had no idea how he knew that.

Lord, give me patience. This situation could become annoying very easily, and patience was not his strongest quality. That thought reminded him of helping pick up the chess set with Liza the night before. He smiled at the memory.

"Amusing sight, is it?" Mr. Fitzpatrick's voice came from behind him in the cabin. Matthew did not flinch. He remained looking out as the older man stumped up behind him.

"Sir?" He kept his voice respectful, not subservient, but polite. He turned to meet the older man's gaze calmly. He did not want Mr. Fitzpatrick to throw him off the claim. Looking at this place in the daylight, he could see how much the odds were stacked against Liza. She was going to need his help, no matter how often this man felt the need to glare at him. He waited.

"Not much, is it, boy? And this is a settled cabin. People come up here their first year, they just throw up a lean-to while they get dug in. I spent two years improving this claim before I sent for Liza. Another year and it'll be proved up and I'll own the title free and clear. It's my legacy for Liza." He pinned Matthew with a steely-eyed look. "I'll not see it wasted."

"I promise not to interfere with your and your daughter's plans for this claim. I am only here to pay off the debt I owe your daughter. Then I'll leave."

Apparently that hadn't been the right thing to say. Those angry blue eyes remained fixed on him. "Did you like the quilt you slept with last night? She made that last winter. Going to be the quilt on her wedding bed. Only the bridegroom never showed up."

It wasn't my fault. He was going to end up having that engraved on his tombstone at this rate. "I am sorry for your daughter's suffering. But I take no responsibility for promises that I have no recollection of making."

"Do you know what kind of a laughingstock you made her? Everyone thinking she'd been abandoned, and her stubbornly clinging to the notion that you were going to keep your word. Now for some reason she thinks it's a good idea to bring you up here. She has faith in you, boy. Make sure you justify it."

Matthew waited until Mr. Fitzpatrick had finished, subtly acknowledging that this was his home ground. "I'll do my best to get the harvest in the barn before the rains come." *Not that I have any idea of what I am going to do afterward, if my memories haven't returned by that point.* "That's the only promise I'm concerned with at this point. I am going to fetch the water. She'll be back soon." He escaped, with the strong feeling that he had only gotten through round one of the match. More was coming, he was certain.

The little kitten followed him down to the stream, and delicately lapped up water while Matthew filled the bucket. Then he splashed cold water on himself, washing his hands and face.

In a way, the older man's anger helped dismiss his last lingering doubts. Her pa wouldn't be so furious if this fiancé story had been invented. So he must really have gotten engaged to Liza. The idea of it still did not quite seem real to him. He had fallen in love with her, wanted to spend a lifetime loving her. And he could remember none of it.

The situation was awkward—staying with a woman who kept expecting him to remember her, and a man who clearly expected him to fail at the first sign of difficulty. But even if Matthew couldn't be Liza's long-lost love, he could at least help her out of her current difficulty. He felt an unexpected determination to stay right where he was and prove that he could make a success of this harvesting. If her pa kept pushing at him, he would just have to push back. Respectfully, but firmly. Lacking a past, all he could do was take control of his present.

By the time he got back to the cabin, Liza had already put on an apron and was busy cooking breakfast. Biscuits, with butter and blackberry jam, and eggs with wild herbs, and smoked salmon. She had pinned her hair up on her head, but dainty little wisps hung down around her face.

She set a plate down for Matthew across the table from her pa rather than next to him. Small mercies. "May I help you with something?"

"No, thank you. I'll get the water boiling for tea. Other than that, it's all ready."

Mr. Fitzpatrick grunted. "Good timing, boy."

"My name is Matthew, or Mr. Dean if you insist on being formal," Matthew said pleasantly.

Liza cut in, "Are you going to say grace, Pa?"

After the blessing was said, Matthew set to eating with a will. Mr. Fitzpatrick flicked a glance at him. "You haven't been eating much lately, have you?"

"I do not recall," Matthew said, his tone mild. "But this food is delicious. You are a good cook," he told Liza.

She flushed, ducking her head. "Thank you," she murmured.

Mr. Fitzpatrick said sourly, "And do you feel up to doing some work today, or are you still too weak from your *injuries*?" He drawled that last word out.

Matthew put down his fork. "I feel fine."

Liza sighed. "Pa, you mentioned something last night when we got home. Something about a gentleman's agreement?"

Mr. Fitzpatrick stabbed his fork down at his smoked salmon. "I don't remember saying anything of the sort."

"Do you remember who it was came by last night? Was it the Baron?"

"He doesn't make social calls. Mr. Brown might have come by."

"Maybe it'll come back to you later." She did not sound hopeful.

"Memories do come back, I'm told." Matthew kept his attention focused on the biscuit he was buttering.

Mr. Fitzpatrick darted him a suspicious glance,

looking for flippancy. He turned back to Liza. "I'll talk to Mr. Brown about it on Sunday while you're at church."

"All right," Liza said reluctantly. "Or you could come *to* the service and then talk to Mr. Brown afterward."

"Humph." Mr. Fitzpatrick stabbed at his eggs as if they were his personal enemy.

"I should like to attend the service," Matthew interposed.

Mr. Fitzpatrick put down his fork and wiped his mouth with his bandanna. "You ever worked on a farm, boy?"

"The name is still Matthew. And I do not recall ever working on a farm, but I'm sure you can understand why I can't promise that I haven't."

"Your hands look like you've done some work." Mr. Fitzpatrick conceded this almost grudgingly. "But you're awfully pale. You look like a fine lady who sits around all day in her parlor, not a farmer."

"He was looking for gold." Liza started clearing up the breakfast dishes. "Maybe he worked down in a mine. And he was a lawyer before he came out on the trail."

"That's hardly fit work to get a man ready to harvest, hunched over chipping at a rock all day long or sitting at a desk reading a book. I probably could do the harvest without him."

Respectfully, as if speaking to a judge, Matthew said, "Yes, I imagine you could, were it not for your injuries. But I don't think looking pale makes me unfit to work. As Plato said, 'Appearance tyrannizes over truth.'"

"You got a lot of fancy book learnin', seemingly. But that don't mean a thing when it comes to getting in the crops. I'm thinking you should just be on your way and leave us be."

"Pa! Honestly!"

"Don't 'honestly' me, my girl. Book learnin' has no place on a farm. Cows don't know Shakespeare from Sheridan."

"No, sir." Matthew kept his tone polite and respectful. "But the beauty of the English language can support a man even in his struggles in the wilderness. As the poet said, 'O brave new world, that has such people in't!'"

Mr. Fitzpatrick seemed to struggle between grudging respect and the stubborn habit of being ornery for nothing but the sake of it. Finally, he got to his feet. "Sitting here all day quoting the bard won't get the crops in from the fields."

Matthew raised his eyebrows. "Am I helping with that endeavor? Or haven't you decided yet?"

Liza opened the door and looked over at Matthew. "Could you go on ahead? I'd like a word with Pa."

"I'll, er, just go see how the kitten is faring."

She nodded her thanks. As he passed by, he said under his breath, "How did I do? Did I win that round?"

She could not keep from smiling, despite her irritation with Pa. "Yes, I think you did."

"Excellent." He looked at her, sympathy in his glance. She felt his support almost as a tangible thing, a rope thrown out to anchor her in a storm. Then he left, and Liza shut the door behind him.

She turned to face Pa and put her hands on her hips. "What were you thinking?"

Pa brushed her concern aside with a wave of his hand. "Bah! A man who can't handle a couple of questions isn't worth fussing over. The question is, what were *you* thinking? What possessed you to bring him down here?"

"Pa, you know I couldn't just leave him. Alone in a strange town with no one who knew his name?"

"What I know is that if you give him the chance, he'll hurt you. I remember you last winter, your face getting more miserable with every passing month and no word from that so-called man of yours. I'd never have treated your ma like that, never."

No, you just dragged her—and me—from town to town until she couldn't go any farther and lay down and died from exhaustion. And then you left me alone, abandoned me, so you could go build us a home out west without me to help you.

Then she felt ashamed of herself. She could not stop the anger surging through her whenever she remembered those times, but that wasn't being fair to Pa. He had done his best. It had not been easy for him. After her mother died, Pa stopped going to church. He apparently could not forgive the Lord for taking his beloved wife from him. She knew he had struggled with drink before she came out west to join him, but he had been fighting that battle. She had thought he was winning it, but after the sight that had met her eyes when she came home yesterday, she was not so sure.

Pa went on. "I can hire more hands. People fresh off the trail are eager to work, earn some coin to tide them over the winter. I've been here long enough that I know most of the people for miles around. Even Hughes respects me and listens when I talk. Not too many people you can say that about." Pa was one of the few men who called the Baron by his name. "And a lot of men have moved down river to that new town that's sprung up, Portland. I can find someone there."

"We don't have time, Pa. The good weather won't last much longer. We need to get the harvest in now. And you know no one around here would help us. They're all afraid of what the Baron might do."

Pa shook his head. "Hughes is not a bad man, deep down. Greedy, not evil. I've known him since I came out here. He and I were some of the first people to settle this far west in the Twality region. He's a hard man, true. Ruthless. But he has a code. There's things he will do and things he won't. He'd never lay a finger on me or mine. I promise you that."

You have made promises to me before. No, she

had to stop thinking things like that. It didn't help. She took a deep breath. "We need Matthew."

Pa's eyes were fixed on her, inspecting her closely. It was an uncomfortable sensation, but she clasped her hands together and met his gaze steadily.

"You're not still thinking he's fixin' to marry you, are you?"

"No." Admitting that fact, even just to Pa, felt like ripping a scab off a barely healed wound. "He's changed. He doesn't remember me now. He doesn't care for me any more than the next woman. I'm a stranger to him."

"Maybe he was never serious about marrying you at all."

She refused to admit that she might have been deluding herself about the love they had shared on the trail. She lifted her chin. "He loved me once. Even if he doesn't any longer."

"Child," her father said gruffly, "if he loved you at all, he loves you still. And if he doesn't, he'll break your heart all over again. You're too soft-hearted, always have been."

"Not any longer," she said fiercely. "I am not the same weak woman he left on the trail."

Pa looked at her with his head tilted to one side, as if weighing her words against the look on her face. To distract him, she added, "But at least he wants to come to church with me on Sunday."

"Humph. Well, if he breaks your heart again, he'll have to deal with me."

"It will work out," Liza said. She was not quite

certain if she were trying to convince Pa or herself. They could do this. Between the two of them, she and Matthew could get the crops harvested before the rains set in.

Assuming that Pa and his "gentleman's agreement" hadn't sold the claim out from under them.

Chapter Six

Liza left Pa sharpening the scythe and went to find Matthew. He wasn't washing up down by the creek or anywhere in sight. She heard the rumble of his deep voice coming from the barn. Curious, she went to investigate.

"Still hungry, even after all that milk? I really do not understand how you expect to get anywhere if you just crouch by that empty dish and cry. Go out there and find some mice! No, don't look at me with those sad eyes. I am impervious to such maudlin sentiment." A heavy sigh. "Here, look, I'll show you. It's simple. Pretend my hand is a mouse. You're hungry. I'm right here. What do you do? You pounce. Yes! Just like that. Let your instinct guide you. No, my hand is not, in actual fact, edible." Another sigh. "Oh, all right. I seem to have saved a bit of salmon from breakfast this morning. I will share it with you."

Slowly, she peeked in around the door. Matthew

was crouched down, lecturing the kitten as seriously as if it were an entire jury. "This is not setting a precedent, do you understand? You need to learn how to hunt."

Round eyed and trusting, the kitten looked back at him just as seriously. It was impossible not to smile, but she hid her mouth behind her hand and coughed.

The kitten scampered behind Matthew as he rose to his feet and dusted off stray bits of hay that clung to his trousers. With great dignity, he said, "He just needs a bit more training."

"Of course."

He nodded in the direction of the cabin. "Has the storm passed?"

"Oh, yes. Pa just needs to let off steam, then he's fine. He'll accept your helping on the claim. I assured him that it was only a temporary arrangement."

Matthew cocked an eyebrow at her. He opened his mouth as if to say something, but he was distracted by the kitten, who had evidently decided that Matthew's leg was a tree that needed to be climbed. Matthew winced. Gently, he picked up the kitten and placed it on his shoulder. It splayed its paws for balance, then settled down. Matthew asked, "What next?"

"Pa is sharpening the scythe. He insists on demonstrating how to use it. It's going to take him a few moments to make it out to the wheat field."

"Can he walk that far?"

"Not easily, but try telling him that. It hurts him, but I figure he needs to prove to himself that he can do it. Don't look at him or pay any attention to him while he's walking out there. He's...very proud."

He nodded. "Independent. That must be where you get it."

She snorted. "Oh, he's much worse than I am." She felt obscurely better, knowing that he understood Pa and his prickly ways. "He hates to rely on others. But this gives me a chance to show you around a bit."

"A Grand Tour? I look forward to it." With a flourish, he opened the barn door and gestured her to precede him.

What was he thinking? It was impossible to tell, impossible not to want to know. As the two of them walked through the fields, she tried to see the claim as he would be seeing it. The valley floor itself was crisscrossed with fields, some fallow, some full of corn or wheat. Liza held her hand out just above the tips of the wheat, almost as tall as she was. The creek ran along in a half circle around the fields. Beyond the creek, the forested hills rose up to the ridge. The little valley was cradled by hills.

She knew she was being foolish, but she still clung to the hope that she could make Matthew love the claim, even if he did not love her any longer. No matter how clear he had made it that there was nothing between them, no future and, as far as he was concerned, no past, a small part of her heart whispered that he might change his mind and decide to stay, but she thrust that thought away instantly. She was not about to get her hopes up when more than likely he would just dash them again. She'd had a few months with him, and then he'd walked away from her and from what they had. Hadn't even sent her a letter. No, better just to accept what she had right now and not form any expectations regarding a future with him. She had her self-respect. It might be a cold comfort, but she hugged it to herself all the same. Safer not to hope.

Even so, his opinion of the claim mattered to her. It mattered a lot.

She gestured over the fields. "Pa claimed 640 acres when he came out here, this whole valley. That was a few years back, before folks got together and started making everything official. These days, a man can only claim 320 acres for himself, or twice that if he's married." She cast him a sidelong look. "Lots of men getting married this year so they can claim that extra land on their wife's behalf."

She had thought—hoped?—that he might take this up, but instead he nodded to the creek that bordered the fields. "And the land on the other side there? That's his, as well?"

"Yes, he owns the land up to the top of the ridge." She hesitated, then went on. "Everything on the other side of the ridge, the Baron owns. He hauls the trees on a road down to the river so he can ship the logs to his mill in Portland." She ran her hand up a stalk of wheat, tracing the full outline of the ripened grain. "That's part of what's been causing the problem with Pa and the Baron. He used to use a road through the hills, but that got washed out by a landslide during the winter rains, and he's having to take a longer route to get his lumber to the river. He keeps saying he needs this claim so he can get better access to the river, but Pa won't sell. This is our home. I'll take you on a walk around later, if you like."

Did he realize that a few years ago this was nothing but forest? They were building a home out here, all their own, with pretty much nothing but their own hands and determination. It took imagination to see what this place was going to look like in another five years.

She looked up to find him watching her closely. "You love it here."

"It's what I've always wanted," she said simply. "A place to settle down."

"Maybe I didn't want that." He looked uneasy. "And that was why I left."

She lifted one shoulder. "Maybe. Your note said you would come back." Her voice went flat, remembering.

This time the silence went on for so long, she thought he wasn't going to reply. Then he said, very low, "I am sorry. I wish I could explain what happened, but I am sorry for your pain."

Well, that was something. It wasn't fair to blame him for something he couldn't even remember doing, but it was hard to stop feeling the resentment, all the same. The apology made her feel a little better.

Even though he was just going to leave her again when the harvest was over. She had to keep that in mind. She was prepared, this time, for him to leave.

She led him through the fields down to the lower wheat field, which bordered the creek itself. The water ran slower here, widening into a pool of clear brown water, dappled with sunlight filtering through the oak trees that hung over the stream. Reeds grew in thick clumps here and there, mirrored in the water. The air was already warm, and the morning sunlight was just reaching over the ridge to the east to slant directly down into the valley.

Pa came hobbling out with his two crutches tucked under one arm, leaning on the scythe with the other. His mouth was set in a firm line, and sweat poured down his reddened face. She knew better than to offer an arm. He loved her, but he never could accept help from her. Not now, and not when he'd abandoned her to build a new life out west.

He sat on a stump and leaned forward to demonstrate the sweeping motion of the scythe. "You're not using the arms to power the movement. Use your legs and your, er, backside." Matthew tried it, and Pa watched him carefully, then nodded. "Try it with the wheat."

Matthew swept the scythe in an arc, and stalks of wheat fell to one side, as neat a windrow as if Pa had done it himself.

Liza had been standing back, not wanting to seem like she was hovering. But she had to ask him, "No headache?"

"Not a bit," he said cheerfully, rubbing the back of his neck.

Pa looked satisfied. "Then you'd best get started. I'll get on with my chores. Fresh fish for supper tonight."

"Pretty sure of yourself," Liza teased. She so dearly wanted to return to an atmosphere where she and Pa weren't arguing. "The fish don't always feel like being caught, I understand."

"Maybe today I'll talk them into it." He winked at her. Then he looked over at Matthew. He cleared his throat. "Well, then." He gave Matthew a last, doubting look before he tucked the crutches under his armpits and swung off up the hill.

"I'm not sure your father entirely trusts me." Matthew squinted after Pa's retreating figure. "He moves pretty quickly on those things."

"Yes, even though it hurts him. He's too impatient. It galls him to be doing what he considers women's work, cooking meals and such, but until his legs are strong enough, he's stuck with chores that can be done round the house. Most afternoons, he makes his way down to the creek. He's got his favorite fishing spot where he likes to go." She wrinkled her nose. "We've been eating a lot of fish lately."

"I don't mind," he said gallantly. "Shall I begin? I can't rely on my memory, but I suspect that I've never done this before."

"Neither have I, not without Pa or someone who's done it themselves."

He looked at her, a crease forming between his

eyebrows. "But surely, you don't mean that you're going to be working out in the fields, as well?"

"There is no one else to help you. Don't you trust me?"

"You are a woman." He was looking at her more severely now, his dark brows drawn together. "It is not fitting for a woman to work out in the fields. It's manual labor."

"That's life in the West," she said simply. "We all do the work that needs doing. Didn't you see the women on our way here yesterday? They were out in the fields right next to their men." When he started to say more, she took a step closer and put a hand on his arm to emphasize her words. "There is no one else. We'll have to get the harvest in between the two of us."

He shook his head, but he could not argue that point. He frowned down at her hand, still resting on his arm. Hurriedly, she removed it, but his expression did not lighten. "Can you at least put on a bonnet? There's no shade."

Enough. She put her hands on her hips. "Look, Mr. high and mighty lawyer, I know you love to argue, but ain't no one paying you to do that at the moment. Let's try getting some work done. I promise to let you argue at me all you like afterward."

"I don't know why I bother arguing with you in the first place. You've been winning all the arguments since I first met you."

The first time I met you, I was crossing a tiny creek and fell in. The water barely came up to my

*knees, but the sun was in my eyes, dazzling me until
I could hardly see. You laughed and fished me out.
You called me a tenderfoot and teased me, and for
a moment I thought you were going to kiss me.*

That was another memory he no longer shared
with her. She turned away. "Let's get started."

Matthew discovered he liked using the scythe.
Gripping the snath, he swept the blade in an arc,
keeping it low to the ground. The cradle attached to
one side of the scythe scooped up the wheat stalks
and laid them out on the ground to his left. Then he
stepped forward and swept the scythe again. Another step, another sweep of the blade. He could
mark his passage through the field by the ever-
lengthening row of stalks lying on the ground on
his left. The kitten watched for a little while, then
went off to explore the bushes along the stream.

Liza followed behind him. She gathered up the
stalks, winding another stalk of wheat around the
bundle and tying it into a knot. He stole a glance at
her. Her fair face was flushed; sweat trickled down
and she wiped her brow, but she did not stop bend-
ing over and gathering up the stalks.

It was laborious work until he developed a
rhythm. At first, he was conscious of the heat of
the sun through the thin cotton of his shirt, of sweat
trickling between his shoulder blades. But soon he
lost awareness of everything but the swish of the
scythe, the sound of birdsong, and the sense that he
was participating in life, becoming part of some-

thing greater than himself. There was a definite feeling of satisfaction when he reached the end of the row and looked back to see what he had accomplished. Here, the results of his efforts were tangible and immediately rewarding, not just searching through dusty tomes for some legal precedent.

The sun was shining directly overhead now. When he lifted his head to squint at it, the light stabbed at him. He rubbed his eyes.

"Are you getting tired?" Liza finished gathering up the last sheaf and straightened. She said, anxiously, "We could sit in the shade to rest. Just for a minute. Please?"

He could've kept going, but she looked so worried, standing there with that little frown between her eyebrows. It bothered him, that frown. He did not want to be responsible for it. "I guess we could take a break, just for a bit."

He sat down with her in the shade of an oak tree whose branches leaned over the stream and accepted the cup of water she poured for him. The water was surprisingly cold for such a warm day. Liza picked up a pail from where it had been half submerged in the stream and produced a couple of hard-boiled eggs and some apples that had been wrapped in a napkin. "How are you feeling?"

She still had that line between her brows. It bothered him, more than he liked, that she was worrying over him. Was she concerned about his health or was she thinking about the harvest? "Don't look so worried. I feel fine. I think we can easily finish this field today."

She lowered her voice, not that there was anyone around to hear. Just the two of them and the sky overhead and the tall stalks of grain all around. "Pa always says it's important to get as much done in the day as you can when it's harvesttime. You never know when it's going to start raining."

Matthew arched his back, stretching his muscles as he looked up at the intensely blue sky overhead. The few clouds that dotted the sky were the purest white. "I think we're safe for the moment."

"It'll be a full moon in a few weeks. Then we'll be able to work late into the night if we need to."

"You harvest by the light of the moon?"

"I forgot. Some people were raised in the city, went off to a fancy-dancy school in Boston and spent their summers gadding around Europe."

Not a spark of recognition or a flicker of famil-iarity. Odd, that he could quote Shakespeare without hesitation but not remember crossing the Atlantic. She might as well have been talking about a stranger. For one thing, he could not imagine walking away from this woman, not if she were his. Or at least, not if he could remember her being his. If he could remember being engaged to Liza, he would have the right to put his arms around her right now as they were sitting here, rest her head on his shoulder and know that she was his and no man could take her from him. He let out a sigh.

"Tired?" Liza asked.

"No, not really." He stretched out his legs in front of him and reached for an apple. His muscles *were* a bit tired, but in a good way, like a body that had been well used for the purpose it was made for. Here, at the end of the day, he could see the results of his efforts. He'd never felt like that sitting in an office all day.

A dusty airless room, surrounded by books, a desk piled high with papers. No matter how long he worked, the level of paperwork never seemed to get any less. Outside in the street, he could hear life going on all around him. Men passing by talking, a woman's laugh. Somewhere, a child singing about robins in the spring. The rattle of wagons as they drove past. Heading west. A vague longing, of feeling like a life not being fully lived, gifts unused, promises unfulfilled. Was he a faithful steward of the talents he had been given? Life was passing him by while he sat in his office and read papers all day.

Yes. That was where it had started—that was what had led him out on the Oregon Trail in the first place. He felt a rush of excitement that he had a piece of his life back, that he remembered something from before that night in Oregon City. A door had opened in that locked room that was his mind. It had only opened a crack, but it was like being in a darkened room and seeing a chink of light. He was going to recover his memory. He would be whole again.

He mentioned this to Liza, and her face lit up with pleasure. "Your memory is coming back! Oh, that is wonderful news. The doctor was right after all. We just need to be patient, and soon you will remember everything."

He wished he could share her faith. Then his dream from this morning came back to him. "I think I remember more about the men who attacked me. I remember asking for directions from people passing by. The first man pointed me in quite the wrong direction. I think…he might have been Mr. Brown. I'm not positive," he added hastily. "I might be confusing a dream with an actual memory. But it feels right." Unless he was letting his innate dislike of Mr. Brown influence him, which was also possible. "It's all supposition. I would hate to go into court with a case that relied on the memories of an injured man."

Despite his doubts, Liza was in a thoughtful mood all afternoon as the sun traveled its arc overhead and began to sink down behind the western ridge. Working to bundle up the last of the wheat sheaves in the row they had just finished, she said, "I know there's still an hour or so of daylight left, but I was thinking this might be a good place to stop."

He looked over at the rest of the wheat still standing tall in the field. She followed his gaze. "Yes, I know. You probably could go on and get more done today. But you don't want to push yourself too far. It's only been a couple days since you were hit on the head and went around fainting all over the place."

"I'm not an invalid," Matthew retorted. "That was just a lack of food, as the doctor said."

Liza looked up at him with such an anxious, pleading look that Matthew relented. He could not refuse when she had that expression on her face. For some reason, it made him feel all unsettled inside, like something was gnawing at his gut. He decided not to analyze the sensation too closely. Some ideas were best left unexplored, safe in the back of his mind. It was just being a gentleman, to yield to her inclination.

"All right, if you wish it. We could stop here for the day."

"Thank you." She flashed a smile at him. There it was again, that troubling, inexplicable urge to touch her, to lift the strand of her hair that had slipped out of her braid. Her hair would feel smooth as silk running through his fingers. He drew back and cleared his throat hastily. "What are you—" His voice came out more harshly than he had intended, and he could see her step back a pace. He gentled his tone and tried again. "What are you thinking?"

"I made a deal with you, to help bring back your memory. I was thinking we could take a walk, I could show you a bit more of the claim than you've seen so far, and I could tell you more about your life. It's already starting to come back, so let's see if we can help you remember more."

And maybe I could remember you? It was certainly worth a try.

Chapter Seven

They left the little kitten curled up under a fern. He opened one eye as they passed him, and then tucked his head back down and went back to sleep.

This time, Liza led Matthew directly up the path that bordered the creek. The path began to climb the western ridge, the water rushing between steep banks. Maple trees were replaced by firs, first a few and then many more, until it felt almost as if he were walking through a green, tree-enclosed tunnel. His footfalls sounded oddly muffled against the mossy ground.

They climbed up to a point where the stream began to narrow, plunging down in its channel. A massive tree had fallen across the stream, its roots sticking straight out across their path. To his surprise, Liza put one foot on a root and began to climb up onto the tree. She moved lightly, graceful as any ballet dancer but completely natural, and utterly unconscious of how lovely she looked.

"Where are you going?"

She reached the trunk of the tree and half turned, balancing on top of it. "I want to show you the highest point of the claim. It's…well, it's rather special to me. I'd like you to see it."

"Careful." A sudden breeze billowed her skirt out around her, and he moved swiftly onto the top of the tree trunk, one hand closing around her arm to steady her.

She smiled up at him. "I'm all right, really."

"Well, you don't want to take chances," he said gruffly. "Don't want people to think you're a tenderfoot."

Her smile faded. She stared at him with a peculiar intensity, as if his words held some deeper meaning. The silence lengthened between them, grew into something else. It was as if she were speaking to him in a language he could not understand. He could feel his face growing warm. Had he offended her? Something was off, at any rate. "I'm sorry," he offered at last. "I don't know why I called you that, exactly."

She turned away. The moment, whatever it had been about, was lost. "It's nothing," she called over her shoulder. "Come on. I want to make it up to the ridge before sunset."

She led him across the stream and up the hill on the other side. The trees at the top stood out as dark columns with the late-afternoon sun slanting between them. Ahead of him, he saw Liza silhouetted against the light, and he stopped in his tracks.

The sunlight caught in her hair, transforming blond into a dazzling whiteness. She looked back at him, standing still on the path. "Come on," she said, laughing at his slowness, and something changed inside him. He forgot about his uncertainties, about the need to regain his memories. All that mattered at that moment was the woman before him. It was the way she gave herself up to full-out laughter, holding nothing back, giving herself over to joy. It sent bubbles of elation surging through his veins.

He bounded up the last few feet of the path to join her.

He stood in a circle of trees—cedars, perhaps, or something similar—that enclosed a small, grassy clearing. The trees were enormous, with trunks straight as pillars that soared up as if reaching toward the sky. Between the tree trunks on the west, he could see open sky; they were on the edge of a ridge, looking out at a glorious scene. The setting sun turned the sky to gold and pink and purple in an almost impossibly pretty display, like a tinted lithograph.

Behind him, the stream rushed down its bed, running over rocks with a liquid, musical sound. Above him, a breeze stirred the trees, moving through the branches like a river rushing over his head. The effect was like standing on a different plane, caught between air and water on an island that floated, detached from the everyday world.

"Isn't it beautiful?" Liza spoke in a hushed voice, as if she were shy, but she was watching him closely.

He could feel her eyes on him. It felt again as if she were trying to tell him something, but not in words. "It reminds me of those churches you used to talk about, the ones in Europe."

He tilted his head, puzzled. "This reminds you of a church?"

"You told me about churches there where the walls went up so high it felt like the men who constructed them were trying to build straight up to heaven. That's what I thought of when I first saw this place."

He angled his head up to study the shafts of light that filtered down through the branches, like light through a stained-glass window. No sound but birdsong and the wind in the trees. He could feel the muscles in his neck and shoulders beginning to relax. He hadn't realized how tensely he'd been holding himself. Once he let his guard down, a memory slipped in.

"Yes," he said slowly. "I do remember going to Europe. I managed to get a scholarship to a school back east. Most of the other students were from Boston, the upper crust of society. I would help them with their schoolwork, and they took me about town. Sometimes I went to visit them during vacations. One summer, they all went off to see the sites of Europe. One of my friends, Ned, his father had wanted me to work for him once I got out of college. That summer, he offered to send me along on their tour. He wanted me to keep an eye on Ned, be a steadying influence. So I did my own Grand Tour."

Liza's lips curved into a smile that sent warmth racing through his body. "You're remembering more and more all the time! You never told me all this before."

He could not help but smile back at her. It felt marvelous to know so much about himself. "I knew I'd seen volcanoes before I came here. We went to Italy. I brought a guidebook and kept reading it to learn about everything I was going to see. They thought that was the most foolish idea they'd ever heard of." His smile faded. He remembered other details about his trip to Europe. That probably was why he hadn't told Liza too much about his trip.

"It doesn't sound as if you had a lot in common with them."

"No, not really. Good fellows, for the most part, but they'd never have to work for anything they wanted. It was all handed to them. Ned, for example, would've gone to work for his father whether he'd passed his exams or not."

"Why didn't you take up the offer from Ned's father to work for him after you finished school?"

"I might have, but..." His brows drew together with the effort of remembering. "Something happened. My mother...my mother got sick." Thinking about his mother brought back his headache. He sighed with exasperation.

Liza reached out, touched his hand lightly. "Don't try to force the memories back. They are starting to come back on their own. You just need to give it time."

He knew she was right, but he really wished she hadn't touched him. The lightest touch, barely grazing his skin with her fingertips, yet still it sent the blood pulsing through his body. Europe. The Grand Tour. He would focus on that. Another memory regained from the treasure room locked up in the back of his mind.

There was another reason he hadn't planned to return east. Ned's sister, Belinda. Newly grown-up, just out of the schoolroom, she had come to Europe with a few of her school friends and her chaperone. They had joined Matthew and Ned for part of their tour through Europe. She had laughed at him and flirted with him, been warm one moment and icily formal the next. He had not known what to think about her, until he saw how she behaved with that young count they had met in Baden-Baden. She had only been using Matthew to sharpen her claws on, playing with him like a cat with a toy, and then she had dropped him and gone off for richer prey. That was when he had realized that beautiful women were not to be trusted. They were interested in the latest fashions and the most prestigious beaux, but little else. Like exotic birds in an ornamental cage, they made a pretty noise but had no idea of what to do with their lives besides being decorative.

Then he had met Liza. He frowned. He still could not remember their meeting…it was just out of his reach, like a word on the tip of his tongue. Still, his memories of Belinda, with all her gilded beauty, faded in comparison to the girl standing beside him now. Liza was more lovely and more…more *alive* somehow. It felt right, walking beside her in this forest, thousands of miles and whole worlds away from his old life. He did not miss it.

His silence seemed to fret her. "I s'pose this doesn't seem like much to you. I mean, you've seen all those fancy places all over Europe. I've never even seen the ocean." She waved her hand toward the setting sun. "Pa says the Pacific Ocean is just over that ridge, or maybe the one after that. Not too far, anyway. No more than a week's ride."

"It does seem strange to come this far across the continent and not go just that much farther."

"Maybe next year, Pa said. I would love to see it. I can't imagine a body of water so wide that you can't see to the other side."

"Can't you just sail down the Columbia to the ocean? The men I was talking to down at the dry goods store, they told me it only took the *Lot Whitcomb* ten hours to reach Oregon City from Astoria. It's bound to be a faster trip downriver."

"I was thinking that if there were even a little left over from the harvest, I could talk Pa into coming with me." She let out a sigh, very softly. "If there is any money left, and if he feels up to traveling."

"I'd come with you." *Where did that spring from?* He saw her eyes grow wide and amended, "Or… you could go with your pa." He needed to keep his distance. He needed to be careful, not make things more complicated than they already were. She was in love with a man he could not even remember.

Liza stared at him. "I thought you were planning to leave as soon as the harvest was in."

He shrugged, trying to act as if his comment had not been all that important. "I don't think there's all that much of a rush. There's still work that needs doing even after the harvest. Until your pa is up and walking around without crutches, I think I could help out."

His easy tone must have reassured her. She said thoughtfully, "I admit, it would make life easier if you stayed. I could ask the neighbors for help, after they finish harvesting their own crops. Problem is, too many of them are single men, and I don't want to feel indebted. I do wish it were January."

"You are tired of summer?"

"A married man can claim twice as much land as a single man. That's the law. But it only holds good until December, do you see? So nobody's going to be pressing me to marry them in January."

I wouldn't be too sure of that. January or June, there must be plenty of men willing to marry this lovely woman, with her hair like ripened wheat and her graceful way of moving. Everything about her was so beautiful, the way she turned her head, the way she put her hands on her hips and stood up to him. The way she fit in his arms when he had caught her on the log, as if she had always belonged there.

She looked around at the clearing. "That's why I like to come up here. Places like this, they're so beautiful that they feel sacred to me, somehow. I come here whenever I am feeling overwhelmed by my troubles."

He could understand that. The birds had fallen silent. All he could hear was the sound of the wind moving through the branches high above and the endless rushing water in the stream bed below. The peace of this little clearing was almost palpable, reaching out to soothe even him. And he needed soothing, needed it badly. His emotions were in turmoil. He wasn't sure what was happening to him, but it was all happening too fast.

Back in the dry goods store, when he had first woken up after being attacked, he had remembered what it would feel like to touch her skin, stroke her hair. Now his emotions seemed to be starting to remember her, as well. It felt natural and right to be with her. Only his mind was still blocked, his memories hidden behind a door that was not only closed, but locked and barred, as well.

And here she was showing him something that mattered to her, and all he could think of was that he needed to hold her in his arms. A clumsy, bumbling fool, no better than a schoolboy. He had to get himself under control.

"This is the most special part of the claim to me. It's like a secret part of myself." She raised her head to look him in the eye. "Do you like it?"

Did he like it? She was dazzling. She was so incredibly beautiful that it was beyond words to express it. It was all he could think of. He had to get himself under control. He turned his back and his hands clenched into fists with the effort of reining in his emotions. He took in a deep breath. "It's very…nice." For the life of him, he couldn't manage anything more. His throat felt clogged with all the words he could not speak to her. Not yet. It was too soon—for both of them.

The more he thought about staying on past the harvest, the more the idea appealed to him. Living on this claim with Liza could be more than a temporary arrangement to help them both out of a difficulty. He had been so wrapped up in his past troubles, he had been blind to his present situation.

Standing there in that circle of trees, he acknowledged what his heart had apparently already decided for him. Even without his memories, he was happy here on the claim. He wanted to stay.

That was impossible, of course. He did not know who he was. With most of his memories still missing, he was only half a man. He could not allow himself to risk becoming emotionally involved with Liza, not while he still could not remember what he had been doing all this time down in California.

He wasn't the man she had fallen in love with. He suspected that the long months apart had turned her memories into an idealized version of the man she had agreed to marry, one without flaws. Her description of their courtship had lacked any signs of two people adjusting to each other's little differences. It had all been sweetness and light. If she weren't desperate for his help, would she even want him in her life as he was now?

Doubt dampened his mood, like a trickle of cold

water down the spine. She might not want him to stay longer. Considering how he had made a clear and public declaration that they were nothing to each other, he could not blame her if she turned him down. It was surprising she was even speaking to him.

He had assumed that the best thing he could do for her was get the harvest in. Perhaps he could offer her more than that. Friendship. He couldn't court her, but he could at least win her trust. He would take things slowly, not rush her. Give her a chance to get to know him as he was now. Maybe then she would want him to stay longer.

Liza cleared her throat, moving to a stake in the ground at the edge of the ridge. "This spot here marks the corner of the claim."

He focused on the land beyond the claim stake and winced. Instead of forest, the land was filled with stumps, raw, ugly, broken-off trees. She followed his gaze. "That is the Baron's land. He hauls the trees to Portland to his mill there. There's a great demand for lumber in California these days."

"I suppose it's necessary," he said reluctantly. "But I would think he would do better to tear out the stumps and plant new trees to replace the ones he's taken."

"I can't imagine this territory ever running short of trees. But yes, it is ugly." She avoided Matthew's eye. "We should be getting back. It will be dark soon."

Coming back down the ridge from her tree refuge, Liza felt as if she were returning to earth after soaring through the skies in a hot-air balloon. For a moment, she had felt as if she had reached the old Matthew, the one who had loved her. There had been a connection, she was sure of it. And then it was gone. She was back with a stranger who turned his back on her.

Her mind returned to his offer to accompany her to the ocean. For a wild moment, she had thought he was making the offer because he wanted to spend time with her. It was more likely that he was only being polite. He must feel sorry for her not having had the chance to travel more. To have crossed the continent, come so close to the edge, and not go all the way? It must sound pathetic to a man who had sailed all the way across the Atlantic and traveled around Europe. Perhaps his offer had been based on pity, offering her a treat the way you would comfort a crying child.

It took an effort to walk upright and not trudge with her shoulders slouched. Her feet felt as if they had lead weights attached to them. She had let herself become vulnerable, shown him the most secret part of her life, bared her soul to him. In response, Matthew had turned away and closed his hands into fists. With that gesture, it was as if a door had closed inside her, shutting off a dream. He could not have been any more clear how he felt about the claim. About her.

If she let him go now, in her heart, then it would be *her* decision. Rather than him abandoning her, she would be letting him go. A small difference in perception, but it would ease the pain a bit. She was tired of other people making the decisions for her. When the time came for him to leave, she would be prepared to let him go.

From now on, she would have to work harder to keep him at a distance emotionally. That was the only way to deal with the ache inside her. She wished he would grow his beard again. That would help. Though she would still have to hear his deep, soothing voice, and notice the crinkle around his eyes when he smiled.

She was going to have to work with him, side by side, until the crops were harvested and the only way she could see to survive that would be to treat him like a stranger. It was hard, but in a curious way the decision brought with it a sense of peace. Matthew's fate was in the Lord's hands. She would accept that. She would have to.

As they reached the level area in front of the cabin, Doc Graham came out and untethered the reins of his chestnut gelding from a nearby stump. "Good evening, Doctor!" Liza called out. "Come to see how well your patient is doing?"

"Yes, indeed. Your father's much the same. Improving slowly, as I said. And what's this?" The doctor took in the scythe that Matthew had picked up on their way back to the cabin, and his eyebrows rose in an expression of almost comical dismay. "You never told me that he's going to stay here and harvest your crops for you, Miz Fitzpatrick. I thought he was just passing through on his way to Portland."

"What does it matter?"

The doctor's face flushed an unbecoming red, and he spoke much quicker than usual. "I didn't mean this kind of backbreaking labor. Using a scythe is much too strenuous. It could be dangerous to a man in your condition."

Matthew rested the scythe on the ground. "You told me to go apply for a job at the lumber mills. Is that any less strenuous than farm work?"

Mr. Fitzpatrick appeared in the cabin doorway, leaning against the door frame. "Boy's got a point," he drawled. "If he's not feeling any effects, who's to say this work is not just as good as any other for him?"

"And he's not," Liza joined in eagerly. "Having any ill effects, I mean." She cast Matthew a beseeching look. "Are you?"

"No. I feel fine."

"Well, then! That's all settled." Clearly, she wanted to end this discussion. "Are you joining us for supper, Doctor? No? Then maybe you'll excuse me if I go help with the meal."

Mr. Fitzpatrick lingered in the doorway a moment longer, eyeing the doctor speculatively. Then he shrugged and went inside, as well.

The doctor barely noticed their departure. He mounted his horse and sat looking down at Matthew. He held his gaze, letting the words sink in. "You should go. It would be for the best." A pause. "Staying here could be bad for your health."

Then he put his heels to his horse's flanks and

headed off down the road, leaving Matthew standing there staring after him.

One more secret I don't hold the key to. He could
only hope it was not a mystery he needed to solve
any time soon. He had enough to deal with as it was.

Chapter Eight

Liza's resolve to keep Matthew at a distance was tested almost immediately. The next morning, she avoided looking at him as they ate breakfast. She cleaned the breakfast things away, and then sat down again to fuss over the little kitten. It batted her hand away when she tried to scritch its ears and nipped playfully at her fingers, but that was better than looking at Matthew.

Pa sharpened the scythe and then swung off on his crutches for his favorite fishing hole. Almost as soon as the door had closed behind him, a bonnet came over her shoulder to dangle down right in front of her face. She picked it up with two fingers. "I believe we have discussed this." The kitten reached out its paws and batted at the bonnet strings.

"You should wear it," Matthew said patiently. "Ladies wear bonnets. You'll get freckles."

Her other hand went to her nose, self-consciously, but she put it back down. Stiffly, she said, "I wear a bonnet when I am in town because it is expected of me. I do not wear one out here because it would be ridiculous. Have you ever tried wearing one of these?"

"Now you are being ridiculous." He picked up the scythe and held the door for her to precede him outside.

"I'm serious." She dropped the offending bonnet on the table. The kitten scampered off into the sunlight, and she followed after it, but the stubborn man went back inside for the bonnet.

Maybe he just needed a little more explanation. As they walked down to the field, she said, "The flounce comes so far forward that you feel like a horse with blinders on."

"Women's fashions are often ridiculous, but there is some merit in wearing a bonnet. It will protect you from the sunlight."

"But I'll be able to see what I'm doing better without it."

"It's not proper for a lady to go bareheaded." They had arrived at the wheat field, the kitten still trailing them, and he handed her the bonnet again.

She squinted up at the sky, then around at the fields on every side. "Whom would I shock?"

"You are not taking into account the feelings of this innocent young kitten. They're very sensitive at that age." One corner of his mouth twitched, as if he were trying to restrain a smile.

"I am starting to wonder about this kitten. No matter how often I offer him food, he never seems hungry. Are you still feeding him snacks at odd hours of the day?"

"I have no idea what you are talking about," he said, straight-faced.

"I think I should name this kitten here Elijah. The ravens must be bringing him food."

"*I* think you are trying to change the subject."

"It is my head, and whether I put a bonnet on it—or not—is my decision." She draped the bonnet over a stump.

Liza knew she was being stubborn on this issue, but it seemed important to make that point clear. He was trying to look out for her, protect her. That was his instinct with women. But he could not have it both ways. He could not protect her at the same time he was planning to leave her.

He'd made it clear it was no concern of his what she did with her life. And that was fine with her. Just fine. Really, she was quite comfortable without him.

If she had learned anything this past year, it was that she could survive without Matthew. Or Pa.

She thought the discussion of the bonnet had been settled. At the end of the day, however, he made it a point to bring the bonnet back with him. "You never know when you might need it. Your good friend Frank might happen to pass by." He raised one eyebrow, giving her a mocking look.

She refused to rise to the bait. "I do not think that is very likely. He has his own affairs."

"Hmm." Matthew did not sound convinced. "Or anyone else might come by. The birds. Squirrels.

Squirrels are easily shocked, you know, sticklers for propriety."

One corner of her mouth turned up before she could stop it. "I can't imagine how you could fail to sway any jury in the land. Very persuasive."

"And yet, you are still bareheaded."

"We Westerners are hard to persuade."

"All right." They were walking along the creek at the point where it slackened its headlong rush, widening into an area of calm water. He picked up a stone and sent it skipping across the pool. A bird startled up from the rushes on the other side, flapping away. Matthew turned to Liza. "Let us try something new. You claim that I taught you how to play chess."

"You did, yes."

"Let's settle this over a game of chess. If I win, you wear the bonnet out in the fields."

"And if I win?"

"You don't have to listen to my persuasive arguments. Not for the next day or so, anyway."

She could not refuse. For once, he looked lighthearted. He was actually smiling. Just a little. And it had been so long since she had seen him in a playful mood. Despite her vow to not let her heart get involved, she could not help smiling back at him. "All right. I agree."

All the same, she was a bit suspicious. He was looking far too pleased with himself as he set up the chessboard that night. It didn't help that her nose had definitely gotten a bit sunburned that afternoon.

Pa, napping by the fireplace, opened one eye to watch Matthew. "No gambling," he warned.

"Certainly not," Matthew agreed. "Just a simple bargain." He winked at Liza.

It wasn't fair. No matter how high she built a wall against him, he always got through her defenses. She couldn't treat him as a complete stranger. Perhaps she should just regard him as a friend. It wasn't as though he were being romantic, after all. This situation was completely different from their relationship on the trail. No hand-holding, no sweet-talking.

She remembered one evening, when old man Harding had tuned up his violin and the younger couples had the energy to dance. The full moon rose, incredibly large and gold tinged, over some unnamed mountain range in Wyoming, providing enough light to see by. Matthew had held her in his arms, and they had danced until they were breathless.

Now she was reduced to arguing with him over millinery. It was a different kind of relationship, not romantic in the least, but in a way, she found she liked arguing with him. That was safe. Playful, not serious. It had been a mistake to take him up to that little clearing on the ridge. Too serious, too honest, too emotional. Perhaps that was why he had turned away from her.

She could come up with a thousand different explanations for his behavior, but the plain fact was that she had laid her heart bare and he had turned away. Rejected the claim and her along with it. Now he was making it clear that he regarded her as nothing more than a friend. Well, that was fine with her. Message understood, clear as any telegraph.

Pa watched them play for a few moments, and then he grunted. "You two can stay up half the night if you've a mind to, but I'm going to go to bed. Got be up bright and early tomorrow morning if we're going to make it to church on time."

Liza looked up. *We?* That sounded as if he meant to attend the service instead of dropping her off as usual. But she didn't want to pressure him, so she changed the subject. "And you'll talk to the Baron after services, find out what Mr. Brown was after when he came by here the other day?"

"I'll talk to him. Likely it wasn't anything important, or I'd have remembered it."

Pa sounded definite, but then, he always did. He would never show any sign of doubt in front of her in any case. Daughters were supposed to be sheltered from the harsh realities of life. She sighed. Sometimes Pa and Matthew had a lot in common.

To her annoyance, one of the other things they had in common was their ability to beat her at chess. Matthew did not even try to hide his satisfaction as he moved his queen into position and announced, "Checkmate."

"Fine. I'll wear my bonnet tomorrow. Will that satisfy you?" She rose to her feet and began putting the chess pieces back in their box.

The puff of laughter that escaped his lips sounded suspiciously like a snort. "Tomorrow is Sunday, remember? You were going to wear your bonnet in any case. You told me that you always wear one in town. No, this means you'll have to wear a bonnet Monday, when we go back out into the fields."

"Humph." She would have to find some other way to preserve her independence around this irritating man.

"Well, good night." He picked up the quilt and moved toward the door.

She placed the chess set on the mantelpiece and turned. "Where are you going?"

"There's enough hay stored up in the loft of the barn that I will be able to bunk down there quite comfortably. It'll be toasty warm. I've slept in worse conditions." He paused. "At least, I think I have."

He probably wants to get as far away from me as he can. "I see. Good night, then."

Matthew reached for the door latch and then paused. Without turning toward her, he cleared his throat. "One more thing. I haven't had any memories come back about why I left you that night without saying goodbye. But I think I can understand why I did it." He took in a breath. He still did not look at her.

Her gut tensed, waiting for the blow to land. He was going to tell her flat out that he must have never loved her.

He spoke in a low tone that barely reached her above the crackling of a log settling down in the fireplace. "I think I must have left you a note because I had to go, and because I would not have been able to say goodbye to you in person. I would not have been able to leave you. I could not bear it."

Then he wrenched the door open and was gone before she could form a reply. The door shut after him, and she heard his footsteps moving off toward the barn, but she did not move. His words had left her emotions in such turmoil that she could not sort them out. *Lord, whatever am I to do with this man? Why have You sent him to me? Help me to find the answers.*

The eastern sky was barely light when they started the trip into town the next day. Pa had slicked back his hair and put on his Sunday-best suit, which she hadn't seen him wear in months.

"Nice bonnet," Matthew said as he handed her onto the seat next to Pa. There was barely room for him to squeeze in next to her. She did not respond to his pleasantry, and he gave her a sharp look. Then he reached out and squeezed her hand, a brief pressure before he released it again.

The gesture helped settle her. She was wound too tightly, thinking about what lay ahead. No matter how often Pa had tried to reassure her that everything was going to be well, she had a bad feeling about his plan to meet with the Baron after the church services. Pa was too honest, too straightforward. Any deal that Mr. Brown had a hand in would be anything but honest.

She had always tried to avoid Mr. Brown. Since the day they had met, she had been repelled by his hot, clammy hands and his sidelong way of smiling at her. Whenever he shook her hand, she had to fight an impulse to wipe it off afterward. Whatever mischief he had been brewing up, it probably was nothing that she couldn't handle—as long as she saw it coming. He had a troublesome habit of going at everything sideways, and she feared that he would spring this on her without giving her any time to prepare.

There was already a long row of wagons drawn up outside the church when Pa halted the horse. Matthew helped Liza down, and offered her his arm. "May I escort you, ma'am?"

Pa stepped forward. "*I* will escort my daughter. People would think you two were courtin'."

Matthew dropped his arm, putting his hands behind his back instead. His cheeks burned red, and he avoided looking Liza in the eye. "My apologies," he mumbled.

She didn't know whether to laugh or to cry. "It doesn't matter. I don't care what people think."

"Your reputation matters to *me*."

"And to me." Pa glared at Matthew, then took Liza's hand and tucked it into the crook of his elbow. She could feel him leaning on her for support, but he was able to hobble along well enough.

She could feel eyes on her back as they proceeded down the aisle. People turned their heads to watch. She tried not to listen to the whisper of voices that sprang up in her wake; she could imagine well enough what they were saying. Instead, she kept her head high and sang the hymns as loud as anyone. Beside her, Matthew's sonorous, deep voice harmonized with her soprano without missing a note. She had almost forgotten how much she had enjoyed singing with Matthew. Pa had a singing voice that would do a bullfrog proud.

The preacher spoke well, and she knew she should have been paying attention, but her mind kept slipping back to that moment in the clearing instead. For just one second, she'd thought that everything might be all right between them once again, that the old Matthew had come back to her—and then in the next instant he had gone again.

People kept leaving her, first Pa, then Matthew. There must be something inside her that drove them off. She felt that old sense of anger at Pa for going off to Oregon without her, at Matthew for leaving her without even saying goodbye. *Lord, please help me to lay this anger aside. I need to let it go.*

After the service had ended, Matthew and Liza waited until most of the people left so that Mr. Fitzpatrick could make his way down the aisle unimpeded. Outside, the congregation milled about. Apparently, this was the one time of the week that anyone had a chance to chat with their neighbors without the pressure of work, and the residents of Oregon City and the surrounding farms took full advantage of it. Liza was quickly surrounded by a swarm of younger men before she'd even gotten to the bottom of the church steps.

Matthew's eyes narrowed as he surveyed the

louts. "Why do all those men want to talk to Liza
so badly?"

Mr. Fitzpatrick snorted. "They're all single."

Matthew scowled. "I thought they'd all heard that
Liza was engaged."

"You apparently made some kind of public declaration at the dry goods store that you had no intention of marrying my daughter. Mavis Boone has the
busiest tongue this side of the Mississippi. I don't
think they're worrying about you."

Well, he'd have to change that. For Liza's sake,
of course. He owed it to her to make sure that she
wasn't pestered by these idiots. He was only being
thoughtful. He made his way to her side, accidentally leaning a bit heavily on the arm of one man
who didn't seem to realize he was blocking Matthew from Liza. She looked over at him with that
sweet smile of hers again. It would have been more
heartening if she hadn't been smiling at those other
men, as well. No wonder the fools were besotted.

"Aren't you going to introduce me to your friend
the Baron? I thought you wanted to talk to him especially."

She stiffened, taking in a deep breath. Then she
nodded. "Yes. We need to get this over with." She
craned her head. "I don't see him anywhere."

Matthew scanned over the heads of the crowd.
"He'd be with Mr. Brown, I imagine. I don't see him
anywhere. But that young woman I met at the dry
goods store is making her way straight toward us."

Liza groaned. "Mavis always has to hear the lat-

est news, so she can make sure she tells it to everyone else."

The other woman pounced on her and Matthew
with obvious glee. "Have you heard? Someone's set
another fire." Her small eyes flickered from Matthew to Liza and back again, prying, trying to read
meaning in how closely they stood together. He
doubted this Mavis was concerned about the fires.
It was just a pretext to talk to them.

"I thought those fires were just the natives burning their fields, like they always do after their harvest," Liza said.

"They weren't growing camas in Mr. Johnstone's
cornfield." Mavis drew herself up, almost bursting
with the importance of being in a position to know
more about gossip than anyone else. "And Doc Graham, there weren't no camas growing in his wagon
when he came out of his house and found it burning."

"Mischief, perhaps? I'm afraid we can't really
discuss it at the moment. We need to go find my pa."

"Oh, he's over talking with Mr. Brown and the
Baron," Mavis said brightly.

"What on earth? Please excuse us." Liza took
Matthew's arm. "We need to speak to them." As
they moved off, she said in an undertone, "I can't
believe Pa slipped off to talk to the Baron without
telling me. This matter concerns me just as much
as it does him. He keeps wanting to shelter me from
anything unpleasant, even if it does mean leaving

me in the dark." She darted a look up at Matthew and then turned away again.

Mr. Fitzpatrick was on the plank sidewalk outside the mercantile store, deep in conversation with the Baron. Mr. Brown hovered in the background, but Liza did not spare him a glance. She narrowed her eyes at her pa.

He acknowledged her with a brief nod before turning to the Baron. "Hughes, have you met my new hired hand?"

The Baron, an older man with a weathered face and a manner as self-possessed as any Boston Brahmin, looked Matthew over. Matthew in his turn looked the other man straight in the eye. Matthew must have passed muster, for the Baron said, "I have not made the gentleman's acquaintance." He extended a hand, and Matthew shook it. "I must confess, I am surprised to see you standing here today. I understood you were quite clear about your need to leave as soon as possible."

"As soon as I have repaid my debt to Miss Fitzpatrick," Matthew corrected. No need to give the man any information about his hope to stay on the claim beyond that. "I am helping the Fitzpatricks get their crops harvested."

"I see." The Baron's tone was difficult to interpret, his expression calm but reserved, as if withholding judgment for the moment. He really did seem to think he was the reigning monarch of this territory.

Mr. Fitzpatrick looked at Liza and then shifted

his eyes away again. "Mr. Brown was just reminding me that our talk the other day...was about putting up a new road across the flat part of our claim,
so Mr. Hughes can haul his logs across our claim
to the main road."

Liza drew in her breath sharply. "Pa, that would
take out the best growing area."

Her pa did not look any more enthused. "I don't
know what I was thinking," he mumbled. "The man
made it sound like a deal that would work out for
both sides. Made sense at the time... I think. And
we need the money."

"We need money at the moment, but we'll earn
it once we harvest the crops. We'll never make this
claim a success if we built a road across the best
farming acreage."

Mr. Brown said, in his insidious, soft voice,
"Your pa made a bargain here. A binding contract."

Matthew said, "Do you have something in writing?"

"It doesn't have to be in writing," Mr. Brown
snapped. An ugly flush stained his cheekbones, and
he narrowed his pale eyes at Matthew. "It was an
agreement between gentlemen." Somehow, his tone
implied that Matthew would not be counted among
that group.

Matthew smiled at the man. This was familiar
ground, arguing a point against an opponent. He
was pleased when his smile seemed to rattle Mr.
Brown more. "It was an idle conversation between
two men. Nothing in writing. Very difficult to pin

down exact recollections of the details in such a conversation. No court would enforce it."

Mr. Brown flushed a still deeper shade of red. Liza, on the other hand, was looking at him with her eyes shining. That made it worth sticking his nose into this affair.

The Baron, surprisingly, was also regarding Matthew with approval. "Your new hired hand has unexpected skills, it seems."

"He's a lawyer," Liza said.

"I was a lawyer," Matthew amended. "I left my practice in Illinois to come out here." Hopefully the other man would not press for more details than that.

The Baron raised his eyebrows a fraction. "Indeed? That is exactly the kind of man we need out in this new territory of ours. Perhaps you could join us in settling an issue." He looked over at Pa. "Abernethy was wanting to get some of the oldest settlers together, present a petition about those mission claims. Do you have a few moments to speak with him?"

Mr. Brown stood straighter. "I've been thinking about that, sir. I have a few thoughts I could share."

The Baron waved a hand. "You go enjoy yourself, Brown. Entertain Miz Fitzpatrick here."

Mr. Brown's mouth turned down at the corners, as if he had just bitten into something unexpectedly sour. "Yes, sir. Good idea, sir. I was hoping to speak to her today."

Standing next to her, Matthew could feel Liza stiffen, though the only visible sign of her disquiet was the way she gripped her hands together at her waist. "If you must."

"I can stay with you, if you'd like." He did not like the hungry expression in Mr. Brown's eyes when he looked at Liza. It made him uneasy.

Liza turned to face him. "There's no need. I can look after myself." She did not actually say *as I did this past year*, but he caught the implication anyway.

Mr. Fitzpatrick tugged at his sleeve. "Might as well let the man have his say. There's no harm in it with all these people milling about."

This was no doubt true, but Matthew didn't think she should have to stand up for herself. He should do something to help her. But Liza had turned away, so Matthew reluctantly allowed himself to be caught up in the wake of her pa and the Baron.

Once inside the mercantile store, however, he positioned himself near the window so that he could still keep an eye on Liza where she stood on the sidewalk facing Mr. Brown. He could rejoin them in just a few steps, if there was a need.

Except that he had only just taken up his watch post when a man spoke to him. "Mr. Dean?" It was Frank Dawson, the sheriff. "There's a man I need you to see. Says he knows you from before, down in California. I think you'll want to talk to him."

Liza remained rigidly upright. Matthew and Pa were just a few steps away. She would keep this conversation short and join them. There was no reason to feel afraid. Nevertheless, a chill crept along her spine as if someone had poured cold water down her back. Being this close to Mr. Brown made her want to scrub her skin until it was raw. She pressed her lips together. "What do you need, Mr. Brown?"

Those oddly pale green eyes studied her intently. "I do not like the idea of that man staying out at your place."

"It's nothing to do with you."

He laid a hand on her arm. She took a step back, but his hold did not loosen. "I was there that morning," Mr. Brown reminded her. "I heard what he told you. He has no intention of marriage. Not the type of man you would wish to associate with, my dear."

"I am not your dear."

"You really expect me to believe that you are still planning to marry that man?" Mr. Brown's voice rose in disbelief. "After he publicly declared that he was going to leave as soon as he could? I'm surprised he hasn't taken off already, made off with all your valuables. He's the sort. Mark my words, one morning you're going to wake up and he'll be gone, with no word or warning."

That sounded ominously like a threat, but she was not about to let him see any sign of fear. Mr. Brown was watching her avidly, lips parted. Odious man. She lifted her head and looked him in the eye. "If and when that happens, I will deal with it then. Excuse me. I need to speak to my pa." She swished her skirts dismissively as she started to move around him toward the mercantile store.

"Wait." He did not lift his hand from her arm. Instead, his grip tightened like a vise.

"This is outrageous. You will release me at once." She kept her chin high, but her heart was beating faster now. For the first time, she had an actual sense of physical danger from this man.

"Not until you have listened to what I have to say." Mr. Brown stepped closer. Dots of sweat gleamed on his upper lip. She could feel the uncomfortable warmth of his breath against her cheek. "Do you think it's easy, keeping my position as the Baron's right-hand man? I've learned to stay on guard, make sure no one comes along who could take it away from me. I've learned to protect my reputation in this town. It's in both our interests that this man leaves as soon as possible. If you permit him to stay on your claim, people will think you are going to marry him. This nonsense must end immediately. You cannot have misunderstood my intentions toward you. I am going to marry you. Not him. Me. You wouldn't want anything to happen to him…the way it did your father."

Chapter Nine

Dawson took Matthew aside. The tips of his absurdly long mustache drooped as he frowned at Matthew. "I didn't want to say anything in front of Liza, get her hopes up or anything, but there's a man who says he might know you. Dirty little miner called Petey, rough as they come. I picked him up last night for being too drunk and disorderly, put him in the cell overnight to sober up. This morning, he saw that poster I'd put up asking for information about you and recognized the sketch I drew. Says he knows you."

Matthew gave a backward look at Liza, but she hadn't moved. She was still standing stiffly erect. Mr. Brown was saying something to her. He did not look as if he were threatening her; they were just having a discussion. Perhaps Matthew *was* overreacting. Even her pa wasn't worried about her.

Even so, it went against the grain to turn his back on her as he headed toward the jail. He would keep this interview as short as he could. "You're keeping the man locked up?"

"Law says he has to stay locked up until he's sober enough to walk without stumbling. Truth is, I could've let him out earlier, but I didn't want to risk him wandering off before I could track you down."

The jail was just a small, barred room in a shed down by the river. Inside a small man lay stretched out on the narrow bed, apparently asleep. The sheriff banged on the bars. "Wake up, you!"

Petey opened one eye and peered blearily at the sheriff. "No need to shout," he croaked. "I can hear you just fine."

"Well, wake up, then. Brought someone to see you."

The miner sat up slowly, swinging his legs off the bed, and eyed Matthew. Matthew looked straight back at him. He had no recollection of ever having seen the man before, but he didn't place much stock in his memory at the moment.

Petey squinted, looking Matthew up and down, then he turned to the sheriff. "Yep, that's him. He looks different, being all clean shaven and such, but that's the man I knew from Dutch Flat."

Matthew frowned. *That* name was familiar. Yes. He had been there. A rough mining town in the Sierra foothills. He could almost remember… His fists clenched, as if he could physically pull the memories from the back of his mind.

"How do you know him?" Dawson asked.

Petey shrugged. "We was coming up on the Siskiyou Trail. I was looking to find some more gold, so I took the Yreka cutoff. He said he was coming straight up here. Said he was done looking for gold. He was fixing to get married." The man eyed Matthew. "Some pretty little thing. Said her hair was all the gold he needed."

"How poetic." Dawson's mustache twitched as if hiding a smile.

Matthew ignored him. He had gained one more nugget of information about himself. He wasn't married. *He wasn't married.* It was one small piece of the puzzle that was his past, but somehow it felt earthshaking. He was free to stay on the claim if he wished—and, more to the point, if Liza wanted him to.

Petey added, "I finally decided to give up on looking for gold and made my way up here. That reminds me. Carter—remember him?—I ran into him down in Salem on my way up here. He mentioned you, something about a letter. He's probably still down in Salem, if you need to get a hold of him."

Matthew nodded his thanks to the miner and Dawson and then excused himself. He needed to share the news with Liza.

Liza stared at Mr. Brown. This could not be happening. "My father was hurt in an accident," she said. Her voice wanted to tremble, but she managed to control it. "You…you caused that tree to fall the wrong way?"

"It's a dangerous undertaking, felling trees." Mr.

Brown watched her avidly, like a hawk checking its intended prey for any sign of weakness. Then he smiled, as if trying to release the tension. "Even an experienced lumberjack cannot always determine which way a tree is going to fall. Of course, I couldn't possibly have done anything to cause that accident. Certainly not. I merely point out that it is very easy for bad things to happen to a man when he's out in the woods alone."

Liza took a step back, wrenching her arm from his grasp. "I do not think there is anything further we need to discuss. Good day to you, sir." He did not move, still blocking her path. "Are you going to be a gentleman and get out of my way? I need to speak to my pa."

"I want you to think about what I said."

Suddenly, Matthew was there, brushing up against Liza's shoulder as he inserted himself between them. His hands were clenched into fists, but when he spoke his voice was very low and calm. "Is there something you need, Mr. Brown?"

For all his calmness, there was a dangerous glint in his eye. Liza was not surprised when Mr. Brown took a step back. He glared at Matthew for a moment, then he turned and walked away without another word spoken. The after-church crowds had dispersed while she had been talking with Mr. Brown. She hadn't noticed how alone they had been.

Liza let her breath out slowly. She could feel the tension ebbing away from her shoulders, and it was only then that she realized how tightly her muscles had been clenched.

Matthew turned to Liza. "Are you all right?" He clasped both her arms, his grip firm and yet at the same time gentle. "You are safe," he said in a low tone.

She could feel the warmth of his hands through the thin calico dress and had to fight against the urge to lean against him, sharing his warmth and his strength. There was something different about him, something in the way he spoke or the way he looked at her. She could not quite decide what it was, but this wasn't the time to stop and figure it out. She merely nodded, and took a step back. "Yes. I am fine. Thank you." She needed to maintain her distance from Matthew, no matter how much she longed to rely on him.

Matthew stepped back and scowled at Mr. Brown's retreating figure as it disappeared around the corner of the livery stables. "I thought your pa said he was safe for you to be around."

"I don't think Pa expected him to act so strangely in the middle of town, where anyone could see. He is—*was*—very careful whenever anyone else was around. Something's changed with him lately. I think—I think he sees you as a threat."

"Really? Good. If he threatens you again, he's going to realize just how much of a threat I can be."

Pa came up to them, and Matthew changed the subject. "Shall we head back?"

"Yes, please." Liza suddenly felt very tired. She

longed to be back in the shelter of their own little valley, away from strangers and their threats.

Matthew handed her into the wagon. For once, she did not protest that she could climb up without assistance. Even an independent woman could appreciate a little help now and then, surely.

Pa clicked to the horse to start. He waited until they were well on the way back to the claim before he turned to Liza. "Lizzy? Is something wrong?"

"I'm not sure," Liza spoke slowly, measuring her words with care. If she told Pa about Mr. Brown's threat, would he even believe her? He had never taken the man seriously, and this sounded too incredible. "I spoke with Mr. Brown while you were off at the mercantile with the Baron and Mr. Abernethy. He—well, Mr. Brown worries me."

"What can Mr. Brown do?" Pa scoffed. "He does what his boss tells him to do, and Mr. Hughes is an honorable man. A cold man, I grant you, but he has a code and he lives by it."

"I do not think Mr. Brown has a code," Liza said, very softly.

"So long as we get the crops harvested, we'll have enough money to survive the winter and pay for seeds for next year."

Matthew reached over and gave her hand a brief, encouraging squeeze. "We will get the crops harvested. Don't worry about that."

"Aye," her pa agreed. "You've been doing a fair enough job on the harvest, I will admit." He eyed

Matthew sidelong. "And…you were a help today, with all that lawyer talk."

Matthew shrugged. "You're welcome."

Liza looked from one of them to the other. Pa and Matthew seemed to regard this episode as over and done with. Maybe there wasn't anything to worry about.

Pa went to bed as soon as the sun had set. He never liked to show weakness, but she knew it cost him an effort to walk as much as he had and stand around talking to the other men after church. Matthew, however, lingered. With a jerk of his head, he indicated the bench outside the cabin. Once she settled down, he sat next to her. It might be her imagination, but it seemed as if he sat a bit closer to her this time.

"I gather that there is more to this Mr. Brown than his just being a man who works for the Baron." Matthew studied her. "What are you not telling me? I can see it in your face. There is something else."

She smiled faintly. "You always did tell me that everything I'm feeling shows in my face. Yes, there is something more I should tell you about Mr. Brown, even if we are no longer— There is something you should know."

This was hard to say. She looked down at her hands, wishing there were something she could do to keep busy. Matthew waited, not moving, not speaking, his dark eyes fixed on her. She had the feeling he wasn't missing any detail, down to the smallest twitch of her little finger, but he said nothing, letting her take the time she needed. She appreciated that kindness.

She took a deep breath. "Over the winter, it got pretty quiet round here. It doesn't really snow much, not like back home, but it was raining most of the time. Roads were too muddy for a wagon, 'less you were wanting to bust an axle. There wasn't too much socializing. Anyway, Mr. Brown started coming by. At first, he came to talk to Pa. That was when the Baron first started having problems with landslides on the road he'd had built, so I think Mr. Brown was trying to see how Pa felt about selling the claim. But then he started talking more to me whenever he came by."

Liza twisted the hem of her apron. Matthew doubted she was even aware that she was doing it. She was staring straight ahead and speaking in a quick, jerky fashion, as if she were trying to expel the memory she was seeing in her mind's eye along with the words she was saying. "I finally realized he was trying to court me, in his own roundabout way. I *told* him I was promised, but things like promises don't hold any weight to him. Finally, I told him to stop coming by. He and Pa had an argument. Then Pa had his accident and broke his legs."

"And Mr. Brown didn't stop coming around," Matthew guessed.

She shook her head. "No. He started coming by when Pa was laid up in bed and I was out doing chores. He is good at sneaking around." She rubbed her hand along the edge of her apron. "I didn't want to tell Pa about what he was up to. Pa was feeling frustrated enough that he couldn't get around like he used to. I try not to let Pa see how I feel about Mr. Brown, but there is just something about that man that makes my skin crawl. He is repulsive."

"I should think he would have behaved better, considering you had told everyone you were engaged."

She gave him a sidelong look. "You were quite clear on that point that morning at the McKays' store. And now Mavis has spread that story all over town." A note of bitterness crept into her tone, and the silence that fell between them felt like an accusation.

He looked down at his hands. "That first day... I think we might truthfully say that I was unwell at the time."

"You said you had no intention of marrying me." Was that the faintest hint of pink on her cheeks? He thought it might be. It was hard to tell in this dim light.

"I had just been hit on the head and dumped in the river. Not thinking clearly. A little confused. Perfectly understandable." He took a deep breath. "I am sorry if I hurt your feelings." There. He had said it. It seemed woefully inadequate.

He hesitated. Liza and her pa weren't aware of his meeting with the miner. Should he tell Liza that he was free to marry? It no longer seemed as simple a decision as it had once been.

He was no longer quite sure of his welcome. She

seemed to have accepted him as a friend and nothing more. What if she no longer wanted his attentions? It would be awkward to remain on the claim if he offered to renew their relationship and she refused. And he could hardly leave her with the harvesting half-done.

He needed some sign that she would still welcome his attentions before he could begin to think about courting her as he was now. Not trying to measure himself up to a man whom he could not remember being. This was his chance to have a new start with Liza. The prospect was exciting, but he had to tread carefully.

"Even if we're not engaged, we are friends." He hoped. "People will get used to seeing me around you. Maybe it won't be enough to keep Mr. Brown away, but it might discourage him from getting too close. And it might help with all those single men who hang around you after church."

Liza's mouth quirked up just a bit, creating an endearing little dimple that he suddenly wanted to touch very badly. "They just want a wife, and any single woman would do. None of them *know* me or care one way or another about me."

"Except Frank Dawson." He shut his mouth and pressed his lips together. *Fool. Don't bring him up.*

"Frank and I are friends, nothing more."

"He wants you to be more than a friend. You must know that."

"I do not care about him that way." She darted him a look, then focused her gaze on her feet. "Not the way a wife should care about a husband. And really, he doesn't care that much about me. He just wants to settle down."

"Well, if Dawson or Brown or any of the other men start to pester you, I want you to tell me about it. This is a problem I could help you with. I *want* to help you. Will you let me?" He knew it was going to be hard for her to accept help from him. She was so concerned that she keep her independence and not rely on him or anyone else for assistance.

He was doing everything he could to keep their relationship as friends, not to pressure her into anything more serious for now. He had shifted to sleeping in the barn so that he would not be distracted by the sight of her with her hair unbound first thing in the morning. Her wearing her bonnet helped, too. The woman had no idea how beautiful she looked with her hair slipping loose from its braid. He was having a hard enough time concentrating whenever she was around. But he could hardly tell her any of that, not until he found a way for her to see him not just as a man she'd loved in the past, but as a man she might be able to love in the future.

He kept going back to that moment crossing the stream, when she had lost her balance and he had caught her. Something important had passed between them at that moment, something he did not quite understand. "It's getting late. We have an early start tomorrow. And don't forget your bonnet."

Liza snorted. "I might have to put up with that bothersome piece of cloth on my head, but don't you go thinking you can start ordering me about. I will find some way to turn this around." Then her lips curled up in amusement, as if she'd just thought of something.

That smile again. Matthew tried not to notice when she did that, but it was driving him crazy. What was going on inside her head that amused her so? He wished he knew. There were times when they understood each other perfectly. They worked in the fields as a team, not needing speech because they understood each other without words. Then there were times like this one, when she was still a complete mystery to him—a mystery he was driven to understand.

Once, he had apparently understood her well enough to ask her to share a life with him. But he wanted Liza to love the man he was now, not some figure from the past. He squashed an irrational feeling of jealousy. *I'm jealous of myself—how's that for a twist.*

"What was it about your fiancé that led you to agree to marry him?"

"It wasn't any one thing. It was a horde of things." Her voice was so soft that it wove seamlessly with the evening breeze that had sprung up, rustling the trees. "Little things that added up to one big yes."

"Can you give me an example?"

"Oh, I don't know. Putting a feeling into words makes me sound so foolish. There was that one time when…" Her voice trailed off, and she blushed.

It maddened him to see her blush at some tender

memory she had shared with that other man who was himself. He was going to drive himself insane. What was it he had said to her, that other man who was his past, that even the memory of it made her blush so sweetly? If he only had the key, perhaps he could win her for himself. Memories tickled at the back of his mind, like an itch he could not scratch.

He really wished he knew what had been behind that smile.

The next morning, Liza came to breakfast with a present for Matthew. "I went down at first light to the pool to pick these rushes." Liza put the woven hat down on the table, half proud and half shy. "I never tried weaving a hat before, but I've seen it done. What do you think?"

Matthew picked it up, turning the hat over in his hands. "It looks very…unique. I suspect the squirrels would approve." He settled little Elijah into the crook of his elbow, where the kitten amused itself by attacking a loose thread on the cuff of his shirt. Matthew plopped the hat on his head. "Tell the truth. Exactly how ridiculous do I look?"

She fought back the urge to smile. "I think there's a time and place for telling the truth, and this isn't it."

"Well, at least I won't have to worry about freckles. I shall make a point to wear it when I'm out in the fields, I promise."

Pa hobbled in from the back room. He took one

look at Matthew and said flat out, "That is the ugliest hat I ever laid eyes on."

"I promised to wear it," Matthew said with dignity.

"And we all know how you are about keeping promises."

"Pa!" Just for once, she and Matthew were not fighting. Would they never have peace in this house?

Pa merely glowered at Matthew and then stumped over to poke at the fire. Matthew looked at Liza. She grimaced, but his playful mood had vanished and his stiff frown was back.

When they walked down to the fields, she tried to explain how it was with Pa. "He wasn't like that before. Growing up, he was the best father you could imagine. Back when my mother was alive. He was full of hope. Too much so, perhaps. Kept moving us to the next town, the next opportunity. We never settled anywhere. I got so tired of moving every year or so. But he loved Mama and she loved him and they were so happy that we just kept going. Until she died. Then, he…slumped. Wouldn't do anything. Stopped going to church. Started to drink. Then he took off for the Oregon Territory, leaving me with my aunt in Iowa."

He frowned thoughtfully. It was odd to see such a serious look under that silly hat. The combination was oddly charming. She had made the hat because she had to prove to him—and more importantly, to herself—that she expected him to treat them both as equals. If she had to wear a foolish hat, then he could, as well.

She was an independent woman; she could survive on her own. She had survived Pa abandoning her. If Matthew left her again, as Pa had left, she could survive.

And he was going to leave her. She had to be prepared for that.

"What did he mean when he said I broke my promise?"

Startled out of her thoughts, Liza said simply, "You were supposed to come back within six months. You stayed away a whole year. No word. No reason why."

He frowned. "I must have written a letter, surely?"

"This isn't like back east. No regular mail service here. Ships drop off mail when they come or the occasional trapper travels up the Siskiyou Trail with a letter. There's talk of getting a regular mail service on the river between here and Salem, but so far I haven't seen any sign of it." She sighed. "Don't mind Pa. I'll have a word with him later."

"No," Matthew said. "I think that he and I need to talk this out between us." He took the scythe from Liza. "You should not have to carry that. It's heavy."

"I am capable, you know. I'm not a frail thing that needs to be protected all the time."

"I don't doubt that you *can* carry it. It just goes against the grain that you should *have* to. A lady should not have to scrimp and save and suffer—"

He stopped walking, and then finished slowly, "As my mother had to."

"Is that another memory come back?"

He nodded. "I remember now. After my father died, she had to go to work to support the two of us. My father hadn't left any money, and she had to take in laundry and clean houses to make enough money for us to get by. I did odd jobs after school, of course, but it was always a struggle to put food on the table and keep a roof over our heads. I got a scholarship and went off to college. She was so proud the day I left. She went with me to the train station and waved her handkerchief until I was out of sight. I was going to come back home right after I graduated, but I got that offer to go to Europe. She insisted that I take it. Said it would be a once-in-a-lifetime experience. But…that meant when she got sick, I wasn't there to take care of her. She had to rely on others to help her. They were good people," he added hastily, "neighbors she'd known for a long time. But they weren't family." He looked down at the scythe, not seeing it. "I got the telegram that she was ill, that I needed to come quickly." His hand clenched around the scythe. "But I wasn't quick enough. I came too late."

She waited a moment, but he did not say anything further. A light breeze bent the tops of the grain stalks, creating a faint rustling sound. Finally, she reached out and put her hand on his arm. "You know that you aren't responsible for her passing."

"That's not the point. She had to scrimp and save

and work hard all her life, and the one time she needed me, I was off enjoying myself." He shook his head, as if to wake himself from his reverie, and his eyes came up to meet hers. "I cannot undo the past, but I can make it a point to help you carry heavy burdens."

"All right," she said. "If it means so much, I will share my burden with you." Spoken out loud, the words seemed to take on an added significance, as if she were making a solemn pledge. This was dangerous ground, and she was not prepared to cross it. She walked on, faster than before.

He caught up with her easily. "It feels as if all we ever do is talk about me. Tell me something about you instead. Where are you from? You don't have your father's accent."

"No, I was born in Missouri," she said, glad for the change of subject. "Mama and Pa came from Ireland, but they couldn't settle down. Every time Pa heard of a new opportunity, a new dream, a new chance to prove himself, we'd pack up and be off again. There was always a new opportunity on the horizon, and this one was going to 'make our fortune.' He would say that each time, and each time Mama would smile at him and say, 'Of course.' They were so happy together, it did not matter to her where they lived."

"But it mattered to you," he guessed.

"Of course! I got tired of uprooting myself on a whim. None of his great opportunities ever came to anything. I don't think it mattered to him. He wanted the dream, not the reality. Then after Mama died, he had nothing to root himself any longer. I think he felt he failed her somehow, so he wanted to make it right even though she was no longer there to see it. So when he heard about land for the taking, he got the idea to come out here and stake a claim. I was glad when he decided to head out west. I just thought that he would take me with him. He needs to cultivate this land for one more year, and then he'll get the title to the claim, free and clear."

"He did all this because of guilt?" Matthew considered this, and shook his head. "You know your father better than I do, of course. But all the same, the man I met—I don't see him coming out here, cutting down trees, wrestling stumps out of the ground and plowing fields just out of a sense of guilt. I think he did it out of love. Have you tried telling him how it made you feel?"

She tossed her head. "There is no need to bring it up again. He knows how I feel."

"I am not sure that he does, actually. If you don't mention it, he might think that you have gotten over your feelings. I don't think you can make feelings go away by trying to bury them or pretending they don't exist. The hurt festers if you don't expose it to the open air and then move on." He stopped. "Sorry. I should leave the sermons to the preacher. He does a better job."

True to his word, Matthew did not bring up the subject again. Over the next few weeks, they fell into a pattern, working from sunup to late afternoon. Then they would walk around the claim while she told him details about his life out on the trail or growing up in Illinois. She liked spending time alone with him, walking by his side in an easy rhythm that felt natural.

Mr. Brown did not come by the claim, and that helped her to relax. Even when they attended church, Mr. Brown stayed in the background and did not join in the socializing after the service.

Her walks with Matthew became a habit that she did not want to break. Liza still insisted on those daily walks, even with the need to get the harvest in as soon as possible. Out loud, she justified the walks for Matthew's health and to give her a chance to remind him of all the events in his past that she could remember. Secretly, she cherished this time with him. It was just an hour before supper. That wasn't too much, was it?

They had managed to bring in most of the crops by now. The grain lay bundled on the barn floor, ready to be threshed and taken to the mill for grinding. The hay was stacked in the loft; the cows would be well fed during the winter. Matthew's once spacious sleeping arrangements had now narrowed down to a small section of the loft. Elijah mewed at the lack of room before he discovered the fun he could have burrowing into the straw. He hadn't returned with a mouse, not yet, but Matthew insisted that he would soon.

Since the harvest had been going so well, she had

decided they could start coming back to the cabin for a cooked lunch rather than eating something cold out in the field.

Perhaps she was being selfish—they should be using that extra hours of daylight to finish the harvest. But the sooner the crops were safe in the barn, the sooner he'd be on his way, as he wished.

He was going to leave her again. It was inevitable. She was clinging on to him, even though she knew that she could never let down her guard against him, never let herself love him freely and openly. Any feelings she might have for him would have to stay hidden in her heart and never be spoken out loud. That was the only way to keep from being hurt. So long as she kept her walls up, it did no harm to spend time with him while she could.

"What an amazing font of information you are," he said one noon as they strolled back to the barn to put the scythe away before lunch. "I must have spent the whole time on the trail talking about myself."

"I liked it," Liza said. "You used to tell the most marvelous stories."

"What an odious man I must have been." Matthew shifted Elijah to his other shoulder. The kitten had adopted a habit of riding on Matthew's shoulder as he walked. Elijah braced his front paws on Matthew's shoulder, and his tail draped around Matthew's neck. "Sounds like I never stopped telling you things. Did I ever bother to listen to you?"

"Of course," she began, indignantly, before she

noticed the upward curve of his mouth. He was actually smiling. When had he stopped scowling all the time? She could not recall when the change occurred. She could not stop herself from smiling back at him. It seemed so natural.

Out of the corner of her eye, she saw a mouse scurry by. The kitten, now busily cleaning his fur, did not notice. Liza opened her mouth to make a remark about Elijah's hunting skills but stopped when she heard the sound of hoofbeats.

Matthew straightened up, pushing back his hat and looking around. Gently, he picked up Elijah and placed him on the ground. The kitten scampered off a few paces to hide behind the bench in front of the cabin.

A horseman came up over the eastern ridge, on the road that led from town. As the man rode closer, she recognized Frank Dawson. Her stomach tightened into a knot. Frank wouldn't come by this late in the day without a good reason.

Matthew placed himself squarely at her shoulder. Whatever was coming, she would not have to face it alone, which was a comfort.

"Ah, Dawson," Matthew drawled. "I mentioned to Liza that you might be stopping by." He gave Liza a significant look.

She ignored it, concentrating on the sheriff. "Frank. This is a surprise. You don't usually stop by to make social calls."

"And I'm not making one now." Frank met

Liza's eyes squarely. "I'm here on business. I'm sorry, but I'm afraid I'm going to have to take this man with me."

Chapter Ten

Matthew raised one eyebrow. "Am I under arrest?" Whatever the sheriff had in mind, Matthew wasn't going anywhere if that meant leaving Liza at the mercy of him and all the other single men in the Oregon Territory.

"What are you talking about, Frank?" Mr. Fitzpatrick appeared in the cabin doorway. He swung his crutches down to join them. "We need the boy to get the harvest in. You charging him with a crime or something?"

"Of course not." Dawson led his horse, a fine black gelding, over to the water trough. The animal plunged its muzzle in the water, scattering drops in all directions.

Mr. Fitzpatrick hobbled over to seat himself on the stump, all the while glaring at the sheriff. "He's not guilty of any crime, so far as I know," Frank said.

"Then to what do I owe the honor of this invitation to accompany you? And where do you wish to take me?"

Dawson looked him over. "I've heard tell of a woman down in Salem claims you're her husband."

Matthew relaxed. This wasn't anything to worry about. According to that miner in town, he hadn't been married a few months ago. "Is that all? She must be mistaken. Or she's trying to take advantage of the fact that I can't remember her. Should be easy enough to disprove."

Mr. Fitzpatrick nodded his head in agreement. "Does she have any proof to back that statement up?"

"That's kinda what I was thinking a trip to Salem might achieve. Find out if she recognizes you, for one thing."

"But if she's lying, she'd lie about that too." This came from Liza, of all people.

Dawson went on, "And if seeing her sparks your memory. Maybe see if she has any kind of marriage license or proof like that."

"Licenses can be forged." Liza was glaring at the sheriff with an impressive scowl on her pretty features. "And how is it exactly that you came to hear of this women? She just decided to stay upriver and complain that her man's gone missing? She should be down here looking for him if she has half a care for him."

Dawson held up a hand as if to stop the attack of words. "All I'm concerned with here is my duty. If there's some woman out there who can lay claim to him, then I'm bound to assist as best I can."

Liza still looked angry. Her face was flushed and more wisps than usual trailed down around her face. It didn't make her look one whit less beautiful. Matthew didn't think anything could make her look less beautiful in his eyes. He turned back to the sheriff. "And how did you come to hear of this woman's plight, then?"

Dawson looked away, shifting his weight from one foot to another. "I heard about her from Mr. Brown. I know—" he interrupted Liza as she started to speak. "I know what you're going to say. I'm not saying I trust the man all that much, either. But don't you see, that doesn't affect the matter. I have to try to get to the bottom of this. And that means taking this man down to Salem with me."

"But there's no call to say you have to take him right away, is there?" Mr. Fitzpatrick had come to stand beside his daughter, aligned in one common purpose. It was touching, Matthew supposed, that both of them wanted him to stay. Even if it was only to get the harvest in, he felt a bit of warmth at the thought that he was not unwelcome.

"That's right!" Liza caught up the idea eagerly. "We can finish getting the harvest in, at least, before you go upriver. Or why not have the woman come here? Truly, Frank, it is odd that the woman would just stay there tamely. If I heard my man was wounded and needed my help, I'd—" She stopped, flushing red.

Matthew hated to say it, but it needed to be said. "Unless the woman were not able to travel? If she were, let us say, in an 'interesting condition,' then she'd want to stay put." He couldn't think of another reason why a strange woman would suddenly decide to claim him as her husband.

Dawson eyed him. "That's more than I know. Could be that she's mistaken you for another man."

"I wasn't married down in California," Matthew said. "You heard that miner. And it's not likely I'd come all this way only to turn aside in Salem and marry someone else."

"What are you talking about? What miner?" Liza said.

"A man I met in town." Matthew looked at her. "I was going to tell you about him, but—" He spread out his hands in apology. "It seemed more important to discuss Mr. Brown." She still looked at him, brows drawn together. Puzzled and a little hurt. "Please. Let us discuss this later," he said, his voice low.

She gave a jerky nod, and he knew she was upset. He dreaded the interview with her later. To the sheriff, she said, "You know rumors are unreliable."

"All I know," Dawson said, inflexible as iron, "is that there's some woman in Salem who might be calling this man husband." He jerked his head at Matthew. "And since he doesn't remember different, it might be true."

"There is no need for you to make him stop

harvesting the crops. It'd take a week to ride there and back."

"I could write to the lawmen in Salem," Dawson said doubtfully. "Assuming I can find someone to carry it, and assuming there's someone down there who can read it." His expression cleared. "I forgot. They're starting up that new steamship, the *Mult-nomah*, to travel upriver to Salem. I can use that." He turned back to Liza and her pa. "All right. I'll send word to Salem that if she can, she should travel here with any proof she might have that she has the right to claim this man."

"That's fair," Liza said.

Reluctantly, Matthew said, "If I need to, I can go down to Salem after the harvest to settle this—unless Liza and her pa need me to help with other work on the claim."

"There's always work on the claim." Mr. Fitzpatrick wore a neutral expression. Matthew could not tell if the older man was in favor of him staying or not.

When he came here, he had thought he would be leaving again as soon as he could. Now, he wasn't sure what he would do if Liza didn't want him to stay. She needed him to help with the harvest and to ward off Mr. Brown. And he needed her. If he had to leave, it would feel as if he were leaving part of himself behind.

Dawson said, "I have to follow this up. You haven't gotten your memory back. There might be folk out there looking for you. I have to do what I can to help. It's my job." Matthew reluctantly acknowledged a touch of grudging admiration for the man. He might be an oaf, but he was an oaf with a sense of duty.

As Dawson rode back over the ridge alone, Liza looked at Matthew and her father, lounging in the doorway. "It could be an honest mistake," she allowed.

"Or he just wants to get me away from here. He doesn't like me hanging around here with you."

Mr. Fitzpatrick banged his crutch against the stump to get their attention. "Before you two get settled into arguing, go wash up. We can discuss this sitting down. My legs aren't getting any better standing here all this time."

Liza cast Matthew one quick look before she turned away to follow her father into the cabin. She was upset, though trying to hide it. He should have told her about the miner, found some way to let her know that he was free without making her feel obligated to renew their engagement. He had to find a way to put things right. Maybe he was too late, again, but he had to try.

Over lunch, Liza went back to the discussion. "I think Frank is honestly trying to help you. He might argue, but he fights his battles out in the open. If he has a problem with you, he'll let you know it."

Matthew couldn't work up any interest in the salmon on his plate. Casually, he scraped the fish into his handkerchief and put it on the floor, where Elijah took care of it speedily.

"No wonder he doesn't want my scraps," Liza murmured.

Matthew ignored that, going back to the original point. "Do you think Mr. Brown is behind this? I wonder if he's been putting pressure on Doc Graham, as well. The doctor was acting strangely the other day when he came by."

"When we were in town, I saw him—Mr. Brown, I mean—talking to Doc Graham. Whatever he was saying left the doc mighty pale."

"So Mr. Brown put pressure on the doctor to get me off the property, then he planted a rumor that sent that benighted oaf—I mean, that ignorant lout, er, I beg your pardon, that fine upstanding lawman—up here to force me out. Is that it?"

Liza nodded. "It's the way he works. The man is like a crab. He never comes at anything head on."

Mr. Fitzpatrick had been listening to their discussion in silence, but now he broke in. "That doesn't make sense. All Mr. Brown wants is to please Barclay Hughes. And Hughes wouldn't stoop to using someone to get you off the claim. He's got a code, and he sticks to it."

"Perhaps if Mr. Brown *is* trying to chase me off, it's personal."

"If he is trying to do something—which I doubt—then all you need do is prove it. Hughes will put a stop to it."

"But how to prove it, that's the thing." Liza got up and began to clear the table.

Matthew rose to his feet. "Let me help you."

"Both of you, out." Mr. Fitzpatrick scowled at them both. "I'm not so feeble that I can't handle a few plates. Be off with you."

As soon as they were outside, Liza turned to Matthew. "Why didn't you tell me about meeting that miner?"

Matthew had spent years being trained in the art of persuasion, first in the classroom and then in the courtroom, until he could sway a whole jury to his way of thinking. Yet here, faced with this woman who had once promised to share the rest of his life, he could not find the right words. He spread his hands out, then fell back on the simplest explanation. "Until I can tell you why I left, then the rest of my past isn't important to you. Or so I thought."

Liza was silent. "I see," she finally said.

He had blundered. He could see that as plainly as if she had shouted the words at him. He wanted to reach out and cradle her face in his hands, give her comfort. He wanted it so badly that he could almost taste it. He knew the feel of her hair, the warmth of her skin against his palms. He longed to put his arm around her waist, draw her close to him and lean her head against his shoulder. He wasn't sure how he was able to describe how this would feel, but he could, with exact precision. He did not dare tell her, however. Not yet. Not until he was sure of how she felt about him. If she no longer wanted him, he would have to accept that. But he had to settle this, one way or another.

"Are you angry with me?"

She turned away, heading back to the cabin. Over her shoulder, she said, "Don't be foolish. You can do what you like."

He caught her arm. "Wait." She wrenched her arm free, and he held both hands up. "I'm sorry. But wait, please. You are angry, clearly. Why can't you just tell me so straight out?" She would never be able to forgive and move on while she was holding on to all this anger and resentment from hurts she had received in the past. He lowered his voice. "Come to the barn with me. I don't want to talk here."

She was still red faced and flushed, but she nodded. "So Pa won't hear."

She followed him down the hill. He waited until they reached the barn door before he turned to her. "I know you're angry with me for not telling you about that miner. You have a right to be upset with me, and maybe with your pa, as well. But you need to let it go. It festers, anger, if you keep feeding it. It burns you more than the other person. Haven't you been hurt enough?"

"You mean like when you left me on the trail?"

That stung, as she had no doubt meant it to. "Perhaps I wanted to provide for you," he muttered.

"Like my father, leaving me so he could build a new future for us."

He hadn't realized before just how badly she had been hurt. Not just by him, but by her father when he had left her to build a new home on his own.

The hurt and anger had festered until it had grown into a barrier between her and anyone who might hurt her again. He ached for the pain he had caused her, by actions he could not explain and did not remember taking. But one thing he was sure of—she had to tear down this wall if she was ever going to move forward with her life. It was safe to live behind barriers, but it was also sterile, stifling. She would never be able to settle down with anyone if she was not willing to risk pain.

Gently, he turned her to face him. He slid his finger under her chin, lifting it so he could look into her eyes. "You are very angry."

She stiffened, taking a step back. She bent her head, turning away to avoid his gaze. "I am fine. I survived."

"By burying your anger so deep you thought you'd never have to deal with it again. That doesn't work. You have to face it and overcome it, with me and with your father."

"I love Pa."

"That doesn't seem to be stopping you from being angry at him at the same time. You need to let the resentment go."

She twisted around to face him. "Are you talking about yourself? Or are you trying to tell me something else?"

"I wasn't the only person you loved who left without saying goodbye," he said gently.

She blinked rapidly, several times. "All I know is that if it means you have to live apart from people who love you, then it's not worth it."

"Don't cry."

"I'm not crying." She blinked again, as if willing the tears away. "I never cry."

He lifted his hand to touch her face, but then he stopped. *If you cry, I'll have to take you in my arms, and it's too soon for that. You're not ready.*

Liza said, "If people want to leave, there's nothing I can do to stop them. Everyone has to rely on themselves."

"It is understandable to be so angry," Matthew said gently.

She folded her arms. "While I appreciate your concern, there is nothing to worry about. I am fine." She wasn't even trying to make her tone convincing, and her attitude was as welcoming as a stone wall.

"No, you're not." His voice lowered, soft as the breeze that rustled the oak leaves behind the cabin.

The only thing he could see to do was help her to face this truth. It would not be comfortable for either of them. He might lose her altogether if he pushed too hard.

Her face was flushed pink. Thankfully, she was no longer blinking away tears. Now she just looked plain mad. That was better. He could handle her being angry. Probably.

"You keep saying that you're leaving. This is not your concern."

You are my concern. But he hesitated, and she went on without waiting for a response. She flung her arms wide, indicating the claim. "I love this claim. This is everything I always wanted, and he went out and got it for me. How can I tell him that he did the right thing in the wrong way? He didn't want me to come out here and work with him to prove up this claim. He wanted to do all the work himself and then hand it over to me." She took a step closer to Matthew. He could see the tears glistening in her eyes. "But what I needed, when my mother died, was *him*. I will never get those years back, and no claim, not even this one, will be able to give me them. Should I tell him that? It won't change anything, but it will hurt him."

"I know," he whispered. "Believe me, I know."

"And then you did the same thing. You left me to go off and make a fortune—for *me*. I cannot tell you how tired I am of men who tell me that they love me only to leave me alone for my own good. You are all fools."

She whirled around, skirts flaring in an arc, and went back up the path to the cabin, where she shut the door behind her with such force that it was almost a slam. Matthew bent his head and closed his eyes tight. Now what was he going to do?

"Well, you made a proper mess of that."

He hadn't heard Mr. Fitzpatrick coming down the path. "Where are your crutches?"

"I can get by without them for a while."

Matthew raised his eyebrows. "Why haven't you told Liza your legs are healing?"

"If she knew my legs were well enough to walk around some, she'd start to wonder why I was letting you do all the harvesting in my place."

"You want me to stay? This is a change from

the man who wanted me off the claim as soon as I showed up."

"I want Liza to figure out what she wants with you." Mr. Fitzpatrick propped himself against the barn and folded his arms. "She needed to spend time with you to do that. I *thought* she had made up her mind. Judging by the way she just stormed off, I'm not so sure. She looks a mite upset."

There was a clod of dirt lying on the ground next to the water trough. Matthew wanted to kick it so hard that it sailed across the yard to the paddock. He shoved his fists into his pockets instead. Giving in to his anger would not help Liza. "She's furious with me."

"Yep."

Matthew looked at him. "Aren't you going to give me a lecture on what a horrible person I am to have treated her so badly?"

"Nope."

"That's a surprise. You've hardly made a secret of how you feel about me."

"I don't mind you," Mr. Fitzpatrick said tranquilly. "Don't 'specially fancy you, either, but that's not my place to say. It's hers. And up until an hour or so ago, I'd have said that she was right fond of you."

"She's too angry to admit that she's angry." Matthew scowled at the other man. "That makes absolutely no sense."

"Aye, she gets like that sometimes. Like her mother, she is. Now, my Katy was a fine lady, love of my life, but she was proud. Didn't want to admit to messy things like being mad."

"She's angry with you, too." For a man who had spent weeks glaring and snapping at him, Mr. Fitzpatrick was strangely calm now. What was it about the Fitzpatricks today? Were they all determined to drive him mad?

Mr. Fitzpatrick nodded. "Aye, she is."

"Doesn't that bother you?"

The other man shrugged. "She'll come round to telling me one of these days. I'll wait. Women need to take their time with these things."

"Very wise," Matthew said sourly. He was in no mood for philosophy. "But what am I to do in the meantime?"

"Ah, that's the very question I was going to ask you. Seems to me that you have some deciding to do."

"What do you mean?"

Mr. Fitzpatrick shook his head, muttering something under his breath. He shuffled his way over to a stump and perched himself on it with a sigh. "This is going to take longer than I thought. You struck me as a man with some kind of a brain, but you're doing a fine impersonation of a sheep at the moment. I can't abide sheep. I mean, what are your intentions toward my daughter?"

Matthew said simply, "I want to help her. I'm not looking to court her." *Not yet, anyway.* "I cannot even remember winning her hand when we first met. I do know this—she needs me now, and I am not going to walk away from her again."

Mr. Fitzpatrick's shoulders relaxed slightly. That was a good sign. "I am not your enemy," Matthew said. "We both want her to be happy. If I stay, she might learn how to forgive me. The last thing I want to do is hurt Liza."

"You hurt her before."

Matthew's throat ached, tight with suppressed emotion that he could not express, would not express. "I seem to have hurt her again," he said evenly. "Apparently, I have a gift for it. Let me see if I can talk to Liza, get her to trust me again. Give me time."

The silence seemed to stretch between them for an eternity. Matthew was conscious of the wind that sprang up, blowing cold down from the hills, the feel of the solid ground under his feet, the pounding of his heart, as if he had risked his whole fortune on striking gold from one unpromising vein. What he would do if her pa refused him, he didn't know. She would always be torn between the two of them if he couldn't forge an alliance with the man.

He tried again. "If I stay here, I can fend off importunate advances from unmarried men such as the sheriff. Or Mr. Brown."

Mr. Fitzpatrick snorted. "I stopped him bothering her before. I can do it again. That boy comes sniffing around her, I'll tan his hide." He looked at Matthew. "That the best reason you have for staying?"

Matthew started to feel as if he were getting his footing in this uncertain conversation. Mr. Fitzpatrick was just another jury. He wanted to be persuaded. "It might help to lessen some pressure to marry off your daughter if I stayed."

"Or it will stop her from moving on in her life. She's already wasted a year waiting for you to come back to her. You mean for her to spend more time just waiting? Or will you let her get over you and move on?"

If he wanted what was best for Liza, then he should let her go? Even that irritating sheriff would probably make her a better husband than a man who had to be told his own name. But that was her choice to make. He would not presume to make it for her.

"Or you could just finish up the harvest and go on down to Portland to work at the lumber mills there." The man was giving him an escape, Matthew realized. He did not have to risk laying out his heart to Liza and having her reject him. He could play it safe, go on with his life. And if he took that route, he would always wonder if she might have said yes.

He shook his head. "I want to stay here. I won't let her down again." The words were out of his mouth before he had time to think. They felt natural. He wanted to stay, not just because Liza needed him, but because *he* needed *her*. He wanted the chance to spend his life with her, not just the space of a summer.

Mr. Fitzpatrick heaved himself to his feet with a

grunt. "You might try telling her that. You're asking her to do all the trusting."

"I'll talk to her," Matthew said. "Assuming she is willing to talk to me."

Up in the loft, Liza grabbed her Bible before heading back down the ladder. As she stepped outside, she could hear Matthew's and Pa's voices, low, down by the barn. She slipped around the corner of the cabin and went off in the opposite direction, up to her refuge, that island of trees on the ridge above the creek. She needed to get away from everyone, get things clear in her own head. She felt pressed upon by everyone's expectations: Pa, Mr. Brown, Frank...now Matthew, as well. She needed to find some peace inside herself.

For once, she was the one doing the leaving. There was a certain degree of satisfaction in that. Though of course Matthew was planning to do some leaving of his own. Again. Otherwise, he surely would have told her about the miner before he was forced to do so.

Her feet found the way, swift and sure, up to the little clearing at the top of the ridge. Long afternoon rays slanted through the trees. She settled down at the base of an immense cedar and opened her Bible to 1 Corinthians. A letter served as a bookmark at the beginning of the thirteenth chapter. Slowly, she unfolded the stiff paper, a page torn from a diary. Matthew's letter to her, a hastily scribbled note before he had left with his new friends for California. She had read the letter so many times, she could recite the words by heart.

Which was fortunate, because there was no way she could read the letter with her eyes blurred with tears. She clenched her eyes shut. She refused to cry. She had not cried since—when? When Matthew left? No, before that. The day she had woken up to find that her father had gone off to the Oregon Territory to build a new life for them—without her. She had vowed that she would not give in to tears again, and she had kept that vow. She was stronger now. She could cope with being left again.

But...at what cost?

For once, the little clearing was not having its soothing effect. There was too much anger inside her, and another dark emotion that she would rather not deal with. Anger, and a sense of betrayal.

It wasn't fair. She had accepted that she and Matthew were nothing but friends, that he was going to move on as soon as the harvest was finished. Then he had charmed her, making her smile, making her incline toward him like a plant seeking the warmth of the sun. He had warmed her life, brought humor and playfulness back to her. And now it turned out that he had been free all this time, he had known it and said nothing to her. He could not have been any plainer if he had shouted his intentions from the top of the ridge. He was not interested in her.

The growing friendship between them had planted a seed of hope in the back of her mind, that perhaps one day he would rediscover his feelings for her. Even though it was hopeless, part of her still wanted him to want her, even that morning when he stood in the middle of the dry goods store and announced that he was leaving as soon as he was able.

For a man with such a glib tongue, he could be downright awkward at some moments—and oddly tongue-tied at others. Maybe he just hadn't known how to tell her about the miner. She could give him the benefit of the doubt.

Tears gathered in her eyes again, blurring her vision. She blinked them away, tracing her finger-tip across his signature at the bottom of the page. She was still clinging to the memory of a man who didn't even remember loving her.

He had been quiet when she'd first seen him on the trail, but once they met and started talking, his stiff formality had relaxed. He had been open and friendly, at least with her. She'd thought they had no secrets between them. He'd been eager to tell her all about himself and wanted to know everything about her. What must his life down in the goldfields have been like to have changed him so much? She could not begin to imagine. Sadly, he probably did not even remember the details himself. But clearly, he had more scars than the ones on his hands. He had been hurt, deep down. *Lord, I know You sent him this burden for a reason, but please let him find himself again.*

He had crept back into her heart despite her best efforts. Or perhaps he had always been there, and wounded pride and fear had blinded her from seeing the truth until it was too late. She felt complete when he was around. And there was no barricade she could build that could prevent her being hurt when he left.

Slowly, the tears began to trickle down her cheeks. They felt hot against her skin.

Liza put her head down on her knees and cried as she had not cried since her mother died. She cried out years of pent-up frustration, loneliness and rage. She cried until there were no more tears left and she was reduced to little, hiccuping breaths.

Eventually, her breathing began to calm, and she looked up. The clearing did not look any different. The sun was a little lower in the sky, perhaps, but otherwise it was unchanged.

She dried her tears, wiping her face with her sleeve. Oddly, she felt better after that outburst, lighter, somehow, as if she had finally put down a burden she had been carrying for months. *It was only my stubborn pride that kept me holding on to all that anger. Matthew was right. I should have said something.*

Not that forgiveness would be easy. It was something she would have to struggle with. *I can do all things through Him who strengthens me.* She folded the letter again and placed it back in the Bible.

"Good afternoon, Miss Fitzpatrick."

Liza jumped. Mr. Brown stood before her, removing his hat, as respectful as any gentleman in church.

She scrambled to stand, her Bible falling to the moss at her feet. Mr. Brown bent to retrieve it. "I apologize if I startled you," he said. He handed her the Bible, giving her that oily little smile that made the hair rise on the back of her neck.

"What are you doing here?" Anger ran through her veins, warming her and driving off the fear. "I thought I made it clear that you were not welcome anywhere on our land."

Disregarding this, he said, "Your eyes are red. I take it you are feeling lonely, now that your swain has left you again." He took a step closer to her.

"My swain? If you are referring to Mr. Dean, he has not gone anywhere." *Not yet*, a voice in the back of her mind whispered.

Mr. Brown had been reaching out to take her hand in his. At her words, he stopped with his hand still outstretched. Then he let it fall. "I understood that the sheriff came to take him down to his wife."

She lifted her chin. "I know of no wife, sir. Mr. Dean is staying on until we can finish the harvest."

A red flush stained his cheeks. He took a step back, practically stuttering his words. "It is completely improper to have that man living under the same roof as his former intended."

"I do not see that it is any concern of yours, sir, but he sleeps in the barn loft. You need not fear for any impropriety. Good day to you."

Mr. Brown took a step closer to her. "What on earth will it take to persuade you that having this man hanging around you is a bad idea?" His eyes searched her face.

His intense scrutiny felt like ants crawling over

her skin. She concentrated on putting the matter in terms that Mr. Brown could understand. "We need him to get the harvest in."

"You don't need him." If anything, Mr. Brown was becoming even more intense. He was practically quivering as he stared at her. "If you agree to sell the claim, I can help you with the harvest. I can get you anything you need. I can supply you with a dozen men who could help you." The look in his eyes was disquieting, but she kept her gaze level as she looked back at him. He went on, "And you wouldn't have them cluttering up your barn, either. You know what I want. Come now, Miss Fitzpatrick—Liza—surely you can see that this is the simplest, most efficient solution?"

"I thank you, but we'll manage. We've almost finished harvesting the crops. I appreciate your concern." Well, no, actually, she didn't, but she was being polite. "We will survive."

He narrowed his eyes in anger. "Miss Fitzpatrick, you have to listen to me!" The man actually sounded desperate. "We can help each other. I can make you happy. It would be the perfect solution to both our problems if we got married. You will come to appreciate me as time goes by. Many couples do not begin with a grand romance, yet they are still perfectly happy with each other. We could be like that." Somehow, he had taken a ring from his pocket, without her noticing, and was offering it to her.

She shrank back as if she had encountered a rattlesnake. "Mr. Brown, let us be honest with each other." Or at least, she would be honest with him. "I am not interested in any sort of relationship with you."

There, that was plain enough. And this had gotten through his preoccupation. She could see the red flush fade from his cheeks, leaving his narrow face pale and wan, like curdled whey. "I think you might want to reconsider this position. You need me."

"I do not need your help with the harvest and I most certainly do not need you for a husband."

"We are perfect for each other," Mr. Brown repeated stubbornly. "You will see that, eventually. Our marriage would unite the two adjoining claims. There would be no more strife with the Baron regarding access. If I marry you, the Baron would never think of replacing me with some college-educated dandy. He values loyalty. And when I've proven my loyalty, he will value me."

The man talked as if this were the dynastic union of two great houses. Except that the Baron was not Mr. Brown's father. It looked as if Mr. Brown preferred to gloss over that fact. Perhaps he thought of the Baron as a father figure. She strongly doubted that the Baron had ever thought of Mr. Brown as anything except an employee. Mr. Brown had no family out here, or anywhere else, as far as Liza had heard. All he had was his dependence on the Baron's good favor.

Unexpectedly, pity welled up inside her. In a horrible way, though, feeling sorry for Mr. Brown did not make him any less repulsive. Liza shook her head, unable to find a way to express her feelings. "No. Good day, sir. Do not come onto my claim again."

She turned then and walked back down the path. She could feel his eyes on her back until she had crossed the stream and was out of sight. Only then did she look back, to be sure that he was not following her. All she could hear was the sound of the water as it rushed over the stones in its bed. The thought that he might still be watching, unseen, hidden by bushes, was unsettling. She hurried on down the path, practically running, until she had passed from the trees and could feel the sun out in the open fields warming her through her thin calico dress. She stopped and drew in a deep breath, looking down at her Bible.

The letter was no longer sticking out. She opened the Bible and fanned the pages, but the letter was gone. It must have fallen out when she dropped the Bible on the ground. Well, it was too late tonight to go look for it. It would keep.

Besides, there were other things she needed to do. Before she lost her courage.

When she got back to the cabin, Pa was sitting outside on the bench, gutting fish for supper. Little Elijah lurked a few paces away, keeping an eye on the pile of fish guts that Pa tossed into a pail at his feet. Pa nodded at her.

She asked, "Is Matthew in the cabin?"

"Nope. He's down by the woodpile, chopping up

wood for the fire. Chopping half the forest, at the rate he was goin'."

She sat down on the bench next to him. Suddenly, it was the most natural thing in the world to lean against his shoulder. "I love you, Pa."

He put down his knife and turned his head to her in surprise. "Why, I love you, too, me darlin'." His arm came around her, heavy and comforting. "Always have, since the day you were born and I held you in my arms." The arm tightened around her in a quick hug. "Always will, to the day I draw my last breath and beyond." He slanted a quick glance down at her. "And you were feeling a sudden need to come tell me that out of the blue for no reason at all?"

She smiled, just a little. "No. It's something I thought I should have told you before. I love you, but—" she took in a deep breath "—it really hurt me when you left me behind and came out here on your own. I know you thought it was no life for a woman—" *which was exactly what Matthew said in his note when* he *left me behind* "—but it's no life at all if I have to live separated from the people I love. So don't leave me behind again, not for anything."

"No, me darlin'." He leaned his head down next to hers. "I'll not be leaving you. But I'm thinking that you might be leaving me."

"What?" She sat upright, loosening his hold so that she could twist around and stare at him. "I'm not leaving you! I never want to leave you."

"It's the natural way of things, dear girl," her father said gently. "I'm thinking you were thinking of settling down with that young man of yours after all."

She was silent for a moment, looking down at the ground. "I was awful to him earlier. I yelled at him. Probably hurt his feelings, like as not. I am not so sure he'll want anything to do with me after that."

"Oh, he will. I've seen the way he looks at you, the way a man wandering in the desert would look at an oasis."

"I've been so angry with him for leaving me. I don't know if I can ever forgive him completely."

"You can," Pa said. "I am sure of it. Your mother forgave me all the times I let her down, and you have her loving spirit."

She paused, and then simply said it out loud. "I do not know what I would do if he left me again." She hoped she could forgive him, but a part of her still wondered. The sheer intensity of the pain she had felt before, as if part of her had been ripped away—what if she was not strong enough to go through that again?

Pa heaved himself to his feet, using his crutch as a lever until he was standing. Then he picked up the plank with the gutted fish. He nodded at a stack of empty moonshine jars. "I emptied those behind the woodshed this afternoon."

She picked up one jar, wondering. "I could always find a use for them. But what—" She swallowed the question.

But he answered it anyway. "That pastor made a good point on Sunday about sharing your problems with the Lord and not hugging them to yourself. I thought I might try it." She stared at him, and he cleared his throat, looking away. "Well, looks like I've got this fish ready to cook for supper. While I'm doing that, maybe you should go have a word with that young man." He nodded toward the woodshed.

"Yes," Liza murmured. Because, really, it was past time that she spoke to Matthew. She had to decide what to do about him.

If he never learned how important he was to her, then she did not have to run the risk that he would reject her. If she didn't tell him that she loved him, she could keep his friendship. That was something, wasn't it? This was real. He had been honest with her about planning to leave. She would be content with his friendship for as long as he stayed.

If she repeated that to herself enough, perhaps she would believe it. Eventually.

Chapter Eleven

Liza made her way around the cabin to the wood-pile in the back. Even if she had not known he was there, she could have found Matthew by the repeated *thwack* of the ax into wood. He stood with his back to her, surrounded by split logs, raising the ax high above his head and preparing to swing it down.

"You've been busy."

Matthew stopped in midswing. He froze for a moment, then lowered the ax and twisted around to face her. Sweat ran down his forehead. He had rolled up his sleeves, and the veins stood out on his forearms. "I beg your pardon?"

"It looks like you've chopped enough wood for the whole winter."

"Oh." He looked around at all the wood as if see-ing it for the first time. "I got into the rhythm of the work and lost track of how much I had done." He leaned the ax against a nearby stump. "I should start stacking this."

She took a moment to look him over. He still looked like a little boy when that one stubborn lock of hair fell over his face, but he had filled out since he came to stay on the claim. He looked healthy now, no longer gaunt but strong. If she had accomplished nothing else, she had at least helped him recover.

"I'm not quite sure how to say this," she began. "So I'll just say it plain. I am sorry that I lost my temper with you."

"I'm not." He bent over and began stacking the split logs into neat piles in the shelter. She suspected he was using this as an excuse not to look at her. His face was flushed. Maybe this was as awkward for him as it was for her.

"You're not sorry I lost my temper?"

"You needed to let go of all that anger. You held on to it so long that the only way it was going to get jolted loose was with an explosion."

"It was rude. You were only trying to help."

"I'm not much good at helping," Matthew said. "But I want to help you. If you want me to."

He was still keeping his head down, avoiding her gaze. She groped for a way to ease the tension. Maybe if she distracted him, he would relax. "I ran into Mr. Brown up at the clearing."

He raised his head, startled into giving her a direct look. "I thought your pa had forbidden him to set foot on your claim again?"

"Maybe he thought, the clearing being right on the boundary, it wouldn't count."

"What did he want?" Matthew was intent, focused on her now.

"He wanted...well...he would consider it a merger."

"He wanted to marry you," Matthew said flatly.

"It was more of a business proposal, not a romantic offer. He also as good as admitted that he had told Frank about that woman in Salem as an excuse to get you off the claim."

She waited, nervously, for him to say something. Do something. Perhaps speak of his own feelings?

Matthew picked up the ax. In one fluid movement, he raised it up and brought it down onto a log with such force that the log split in two. Wood chips flew in all directions. "I don't like the idea of that man coming onto your claim anytime he thinks he can. Maybe if I stayed on here to help, he might stay away."

"Stayed on to help?"

"After the harvest, I mean. Do you think you might need some additional help on the claim after that?" He kept his eyes on the ax, frowning at it.

"Pa's legs aren't healing as fast as they should," Liza admitted. Was Matthew offering to stay out of pity or was it because he wanted to stay with her? "He might need help after the harvest is done."

"Just your pa?" The words were spoken so softly, she almost missed them.

This conversation was venturing onto dangerous ground. She wasn't ready to risk telling him how she felt about him. Not yet. She needed time. "Let's get through the harvest before we decide anything else."

"All right." He still did not look at her.

"You don't sound as if it is all right. Do you not want to help with the harvesting any longer?"

"It's not that. Of course it's a good idea. I want to stay here on the claim. You need me. And I like the work. It's just—" Restlessly, he began stacking the wood again. "I should have been there with you." The words burst out of him. "I should have been there, protected you from him. I do not like the idea of that man alone with you."

"Well, I can't say that I like it, either. He makes my skin crawl. But if he thinks I'm already engaged, he can't expect me to marry him." This conversation was going all wrong again, and she wasn't sure how to make it right. She sighed, feeling suddenly very tired. "Look, that's more than enough wood for tonight, all right? I'll help you carry it."

"Women doing manual labor," he muttered.

"Life in the West," she replied.

She piled up the firewood next to the cabin door. "There's still a little time before Pa has supper ready. We need to take a walk."

She wasn't sure if it was something she had said that had plunged Matthew into gloom or if this was one of his dark moods. In either case, she needed to put things right between them. Or at least she needed to try.

He piled his stack of wood next to hers, and they set off down the hill. There wasn't enough light left to go up to the little clearing, but they could at least walk down to the pool. Matthew walked at her side without speaking, his hands clasped behind his back.

Liza cast a sidelong glance at him. His expression looked remote, his thoughts far away, somewhere dark. He used to fall into moods like this from time to time while they were on the trail. The best way to deal with the gloom was not to try to cheer him up, but to stay nearby. He just needed to know he was not alone.

"What are you thinking?"

"I was just remembering Vince. He was a friend I made in California."

"Another memory has come back." Liza would have been more cheered by this news if Matthew hadn't seemed so sad about it. "What did you remember?"

Matthew hesitated. Then he went on, the words coming reluctantly. "Vince was my partner. I met him in Dutch Flat and we hit it off, so we teamed up. We did well, for a while. Struck it rich, found a vein that made us a lot of gold. We were bringing it into town when these men jumped us."

The words tumbled out of him unbidden, almost as if he were reliving the nightmare. "They took everything we had, except for the nugget I'd hidden in my boot. Just enough gold for a couple of rings." He cleared his throat. "I was knocked out, and when I came to, everything was gone. There was just Vince lying there bleeding in the dirt. It took me a while to find a doctor. I carried him through the town, just as it was getting dark, never knowing if the robbers were going to catch up with us and finish the job. Finally got him to the doc, but I was too late."

She stopped walking. They were just at the edge of the cornfield, where the ground began to slope down toward the stream. He stopped with her and turned his head inquiringly.

"You do know that it wasn't your fault, don't you?"

He raised his eyebrows. "Do I? What I know is that I was too late. Vince died. If I had gotten him to the doctor sooner, he might have lived. Yes, I know, he might have died anyway. I'll never know now. There might have been a chance." Something in her face caused him to smile, just a little. "I am not very good company sometimes. I can't help it. That's how I feel."

"Never apologize for being honest." She tucked her hand under his arm and nestled against his shoulder. He froze. She could feel his heartbeat beneath the thin linen of his shirt. Her own heart was beating like a jackrabbit in full flight. He was warm, smelling very slightly of sweat and cedar.

She straightened up. She had reached out to him on impulse, to ease his pain. She could not stand there and witness his suffering without doing something. He mattered too much. A friend could do that, couldn't she?

She hadn't expected that holding him like this would give her a strong sense of contentment. For a moment, she even dared picture a life with him, chasing young children with dark eyes all over the valley, watching them climb trees and train kittens… When she drew back from him, she was still smiling. She could not help it. She could so exactly picture what his children would look like.

"What on earth are you smiling at?" He shook his head at her. "Women. I will never understand women."

"Come on." She tugged at his arm. "Pa's going to give our supper to the kitten if we don't get back."

Matthew walked back to the cabin with Liza. It felt natural to walk like this with her, side by side, just as they had on the trail.

Just as they had on the trail.

He stopped dead in his tracks.

This wasn't a door opening in his mind. This was a floodgate. Memories swirled through him until he was drowning in them. And all of Liza: sitting there in the middle of that shallow stream, soaked to the waist and not even caring, just laughing up at him as he called her a tenderfoot. Stretching her hands out to him as they danced with a full moon lighting the snowy mountains somewhere in Wyoming. Sitting beside him by the campfire while he told her stories of his life back east. Liza. By his side all those days and weeks as they had crossed the continent together. Of course he loved her. He had always loved her, with every ounce of certainty in him, this woman who walked beside him.

Liza looked around and caught him staring at her. "What's wrong?" He shook his head, too full of words to speak. He didn't know where to begin to explain the emotions swirling through him. She blushed a concentrated red. "Sorry. I did not mean to pry. You have the right to your privacy." She walked back to the cabin ahead of him.

He had done that to her, made her reluctant to show any sign of affection toward him. Because she thought he didn't care for her any longer. Or maybe it was her way of acknowledging that things were different now. They were no more than friends. He couldn't blame her if that were the case, but he wanted her to give him a chance to make it up to her, to make things right between them. She thought he was offering to stay on merely because her pa needed his help. Had he been unclear, or was she trying to avoid any kind of romantic entanglements?

Had he, yet again, come too late?

The rest of the evening passed in a blur. Matthew ate the food put in front of him and answered when spoken to, but his mind was busy putting together the puzzle of his past. He did not have all the pieces. He did not remember leaving Liza at Fort Hall, or much about his life in California, but he had recovered enough of his memories to know that he could go forward. He could bare his heart to Liza, ask her to commit to him again. Not just let him stay on as a friend to protect her from people like Mr. Brown, but marriage. Settling down with him. They could build a little extension to the cabin, make it more of a home. Their home.

He had to be careful, though. He had hurt her,

first by leaving so abruptly and then again when he hadn't recognized her when he came back. He couldn't help what had happened in the past. But he could make sure he did not repeat his mistakes.

He hesitated, and then decided not to tell Liza what he was remembering. Not quite yet. He needed to be sure she would welcome him back. He had planned to open his heart to her that night, to tell her all his feelings, before she had distracted him with that disturbing picture of Mr. Brown wandering onto the claim whenever the mood took him. And now he had to sort through this horde of returned memories. Could he use them to help him win her back?

How had he wooed her before? It had all seemed so simple then, so natural. He had fallen back into the pattern of walking with her every day. That was a good start. He remembered telling her tales of his past life. But he suspected that she knew all of his tales by now. That wasn't what had drawn her to him. What was it? He racked his memory.

He was going to do things right this time. Prepare as if it were the most important court case of his life and choose his ground carefully. Sunday, after church, if Mr. Fitzpatrick didn't mind spending a little more time than usual with his cronies, Matthew could take Liza for a walk in town, court her properly and tell her that he remembered the time they spent together on the trail. Yes. That sounded like a good plan.

* * *

Liza woke early the next morning. She felt clear-headed and refreshed. She knew what she had to do. She was being a coward, settling for friendship when she wanted more. The worst thing Matthew could do was say no, and then at least she would know where she stood with him. The best approach would be to let him know she wanted a chance for them to grow together, but not to make him feel forced or pressured.

Shyly, she confessed this to Pa when she went down to make the morning tea. Matthew was still in the barn, and they were alone. "After the service today, I thought I would tell Matthew…that I'd like him to stay longer. Spend the winter, at least. I know we had originally said he'd stay until the harvest was done, but I've changed my mind." She summoned the courage to peer up at her father, but his face was noncommittal. "Do you mind? I know you said he'd hurt me, but I still want to try to make things work out between us." She half smiled. "I understand if you need to tell me I'm a fool."

"Aye, you're a fool, my daughter." His arm came around her in a quick hug, and then he stood back and looked down at her. Despite his words, he was smiling. "But you're the best kind of fool. I'm proud of you."

"Then it's settled. I'll speak to Matthew after church services today." She went to fetch her fancy bonnet, the one with the blue satin ribbon. It always made her feel as if she were a horse with blinders on, but people said it flattered her. She wanted to look her best. This was going to be a special day.

After breakfast, while Liza went down to feed the chickens, Matthew drew Mr. Fitzpatrick aside for a private word.

"After the service today, I want to ask Liza if she will marry me. I know that I don't have all my memories back yet, but I do remember that I was not able to ask you for your blessing before I asked Liza for her hand. I would like to ask you now."

Her pa had the oddest look on his face. He coughed a bit, and his face was definitely red, as if holding something back. Laughter? What on earth could he possibly find funny in this situation? "Of course, I understand if you think I'm acting too soon." Matthew understood nothing of the sort, but he was trying to be diplomatic He was sure the man *was* laughing at him. "What is the matter? Do you think Liza and I would not make a good match of it?"

"No." Mr. Fitzpatrick wiped his eyes and straightened up. "No, on the contrary. I think you and Liza are well matched indeed." He slapped Matthew on the back. "Yes, it is time to ask her to marry you." He hobbled off, leaving Matthew frowning after him. Well, at least that wasn't a refusal. Maybe someday he would find out what all that was about. He went to harness up the horse.

On the wagon ride into town, he noticed Mr.

Fitzpatrick looking up and frowning. "Is something wrong?"

"I don't like the look of that sky. We've had a good streak with the sunny weather these past weeks. But the wind's shifted to the west, and that usually means a storm is coming."

"Do we need to worry?" Liza asked, smiling. "We've almost got the last of the wheat in. Only another day of work and we will be finished. It doesn't look like rain just yet."

"I hope so," Mr. Fitzpatrick said heavily.

All through the service, Matthew stood when the others stood, sang the hymns with Liza harmonizing at his side, sat and listened to the sermon. He went through the motions, but his mind was racing ahead to the moment afterward. The moment when he was going to ask Liza to agree to marry him—again.

He knew what he wanted. There were times, this past week, when he had caught her looking at him. Not frowning, not smiling, just an intense look. As soon as she felt his gaze, she would look away. He had never considered her shy before.

It had not been this hard to contemplate matrimony the first time he had proposed to her. Then, he had been full of confidence. Now he was full of questions. He had hurt her, badly. Too badly to trust him again?

The service was over. Everyone stood up and began to make their way to the door. His stomach tightened. This was it.

Outside the door, he took Liza by the elbow.

"Could I speak to you? Somewhere a little quieter. Over by the Ermatingers' house. There's something I need to ask you."

"Excellent," she said. "I need to ask you something, as well."

He stopped in the shadow of an elm tree. They were still within sight of the church, but they were out of earshot of the congregation chatting outside.

Liza glanced behind Matthew and grimaced.

"Is something wrong?"

"Nothing really," she said. "I saw Mr. Brown and Frank looking our way. Maybe we should go somewhere more private."

"I don't think Mr. Brown will bother you any longer," Matthew said. He took both her hands in his. "I wanted to ask you something. I wonder if you might consider…changing our agreement slightly."

"Very well," Liza said. "What part of our agreement did you want to change?"

"The part about it being temporary," Matthew said. He took a breath. "Liza, I wonder if you would do me the honor of—"

"Ah, there you are." Frank came to a stop in front of them. "Excellent timing."

Liza's eyebrows twitched together. "Frank, it's lovely to see you, but this isn't the best time for a chat."

"I'm not here on a social call, Liza." Frank stepped aside, revealing a small, dark-haired woman standing behind him. "I've brought someone to meet you."

Matthew released Liza's hands and turned to face the woman, frowning. "Have we met? You seem familiar, somehow."

"I should hope so," the woman said. And then she added, "Darling."

Chapter Twelve

Liza had never seen Matthew look so grim. His thick eyebrows were drawn together, and his dark eyes held no trace of warmth. If he had scowled at her like that, she would have taken a step back. The dark-haired woman just gave him a little smile, like a cat who had swallowed all the cream.

Very quietly, Matthew said, "Why did you call me that?"

She lowered her eyelashes demurely. "That's what I've always called you, since our marriage."

Frank broke in. "Mrs. Dean—that is to say, this woman—came to see me after the service. She says she recognized you right away. And you remember her, too, seems like."

"No..." Matthew shook his head, then corrected himself scrupulously. "She looks familiar, but I'm sure that I never married the woman."

"It's all right," the woman soothed. She came a step closer, raising her hand as if to place it on his chest. Then she looked up at his face, the narrowed eyes and the lips compressed into a thin line, and her hand dropped to her side. "I don't expect you to remember everything right away. It is something that you can remember me at all. The rest will come back, given time."

"I'm obliged for your kindness. Perhaps you could further oblige me by answering a few questions." Now Matthew was the silken-voiced lawyer, softening his approach to set the witness at ease. "When did we first meet? And where?"

"I met you on the Siskiyou Trail. My husband was a miner. After I lost him, you...comforted me." The eyelashes swept down, and then she raised her eyes up to meet his, and she smiled. "You were very comforting."

"Indeed." Matthew's face was immobile, showing no emotion apart from the intense look in his dark eyes. "So, we met and decided to get married, just like that."

A faint chuckle escaped her red lips. "I believe you were concerned that we not anticipate our wedding evening. You gave me a lovely ring." She waved it under his nose. "See?"

"And I just happened to have a wedding ring with me, out in the middle of the wilderness?" Matthew asked quietly.

For the first time, she hesitated. Then she went on, a touch defiantly, "Yes. You did." She twisted the ring on her finger, tugging on it a little.

"It looks a little small for you," he observed.

"It's fine." She could not quite control the grimace as she tried to push it farther down onto her finger. "My fingers are a bit swollen." She opened up a little reticule looped around her wrist and peered inside. "I brought your ring, too…ah, here it is." She produced a plain gold band. "You left it with me so it wouldn't get stolen. Here, I'll put it on."

Liza watched in disbelief as the ring slipped easily over Matthew's finger. The woman beamed up at him. "That one fits."

He looked down at the ring. "Yes," he said slowly. "I remember putting this on." His eyes came back up to look at the woman, and for the first time, Liza could see doubt in his eyes.

She did not know what to think of the woman's story. The woman did not seem mad or drunk. She was neatly dressed in an outfit of plum-colored velvet with black accents. Her black bonnet was lined with ruched lavender velvet with a braided black trim. She stood at ease, smiling a self-satisfied little smile up at Matthew. But Liza could not grasp the woman's words. How could Matthew have possibly married her? He had been concerned with what he might have done while he was down in California. But not this. It did not seem possible.

Yet as the woman told her story, her words planted a seed of doubt into Liza's mind that began to bloom into a dreadful certainty. It could be the truth. The woman's tale made a twisted kind of sense. Matthew was always so concerned with protecting women. She could see an unscrupulous woman taking advantage of his better nature, using his sense of chivalry to trap him into a marriage he did not want. And then, of course, he *would* feel obliged to come up to Oregon to tell her what had happened. That all fit in with what she knew of him. For one horrible black moment, she believed the woman's story. Then she blinked and focused on the woman in front of her.

Something wasn't right here. She could not quite put her finger on it, but there was something about the woman. Some detail nagged at her. Perhaps it was her body language, the way she stood, leaning forward on her toes, the way she watched Matthew. She was too eager. Pushing him to believe her. She was not as sure of herself as Liza had thought at first.

She could not remain silent. "You had a proper marriage? With a pastor and everything? Including a license?"

The woman did not even bother looking in Liza's direction; neither did she respond.

Matthew repeated, "You have a marriage license?"

"Of course." The woman smiled at him. "I brought it with me." From her reticule, the woman withdrew a piece of stiff paper that crackled as she unfolded it. Liza could see the fancy scrollwork across the top that proclaimed, Marriage License.

"Adeline Beaumont." Matthew pronounced the name in a doubtful tone. "I see."

Mr. Brown appeared at her side. Startled, Liza jumped back, and Matthew turned, his hand sliding under her elbow to support her. "Are you all right?" She nodded, and he let his hand drop. She missed his touch as soon as he released her.

Mr. Brown beamed at her. "So sorry to startle you, Miss Fitzpatrick. I note that the marriage license has Mr. Dean's signature on it. It matches perfectly with that letter he wrote you." He flourished the letter.

"What letter?" Matthew asked. He examined the signature on his letter, comparing it to the signature on the license. "It could be an imitation," he said finally. "A very good one."

"I dropped that letter in the clearing," Liza said in a small voice. "I did not think that he would stoop to stealing it from me. I would like it back now, please."

"Of course." Matthew handed it to her. He went back to the license. "This was signed in Salem."

Mr. Brown's smile faded slightly. "What of it?"

"That means there will be a record of the marriage there, if anyone bothered to go down to Salem."

"Come now," Mr. Brown said in the lordly tone of a man enjoying the moral high ground. "Quit stalling. Admit your responsibilities, man."

The woman lowered her eyes, twisting the ring on her finger. "I can't believe you're doubting my word, after all we've been to each other."

Matthew shifted, uncomfortable. "Perhaps you might be more comfortable with the ring off, ma'am," he said gently.

"Call me Addy," the woman said. She tugged the ring until it came off her finger, but when he reached out his hand, she dropped it in her reticule. "I just need to have the size adjusted. I'll find someone who can do the work."

He frowned at her. "You have a place to stay? Enough money to live on?"

"You gave me enough to live on for a while. You said you were just going up to Oregon City to take care of some trivial business and then you'd come back to me. I know you'd never leave me permanently, but—" the woman lowered her lashes for a moment "—it gets a bit lonely."

"I'm just concerned that you are not destitute," he said crisply.

Pa came over to join them. He cast a glance around at the circle of interested faces who had gathered to listen. "Maybe we should be having this discussion somewhere a little less…crowded."

Liza could not have agreed more. The woman had timed her attack perfectly. With that interested audience all around, Matthew was being put on trial in the court of public opinion.

"There is no need for any further discussion," Matthew said. He raised his head, pitching his voice so that it carried to the interested spectators. "For the record, and in front of these witnesses, I promise all of you that I have no recollection of marrying this woman."

"Oh, darling." From her reticule, Addy produced a handkerchief and began dabbing at her perfectly dry eyes. "It breaks my heart to hear you talk like that."

"Now, now." Frank looked alarmed. "No need to cry. You're feeling a bit tired. Maybe you should go to the hotel and get a cup of tea." He looked even more alarmed when the woman clutched his arm, still holding the handkerchief up to her eyes, but he bravely shepherded her off in the direction of the hotel. Matthew stared after them.

Mr. Brown said to Liza, "Perhaps we should leave your hired hand to deal with his own affairs. It is a private matter between the two of them."

Liza raised her chin as she faced Mr. Brown. "I rather think it concerns me, as well."

"Of course." Matthew roused from his thoughts. "I promised you that I would get the harvest in. That job is not yet done."

"Almost done," Pa conceded.

"And once he's gone," Mr. Brown said to Liza, "we may discuss our future."

"We have no future," Liza said. "With the crops safe in the barn, Pa and I will be able to stay on the claim all winter. And Matthew can stay as long as he likes."

Mr. Brown stared, the amusement fading from his expression. "I don't believe this. You can't still want him to stay. What will it take for you to come to your senses? Addy is going to spread that tale to everyone who will listen. Are you so blind…" He stopped, and began again, his voice soft and implacable. "Miss Fitzpatrick, I think you might want to reconsider your position. It is obvious that your hired hand has been, shall we say, carrying on with other women. He's not the sort of man you want on your claim. I, on the other hand, can ensure that you and your father are comfortably situated after the Baron has taken over your claim."

Matthew stepped between Mr. Brown and Liza. Pa didn't move, his body tense, eyes flickering between Mr. Brown and Matthew. One of his fists clenched and unclenched.

Mr. Brown's hand twitched as though he too were about to make a fist. Softly, he said, "We will conclude this discussion another time."

"You say one more word," Pa said calmly, "and I'll swear out a complaint against you. Hughes won't stand by you then, I can assure you. The last thing he wants is a public scandal."

This threat struck home. Mr. Brown went very pale. He opened his mouth to say something, then he shut it again. He stared at Pa, then Matthew. He stared at Liza the longest of all. Then he turned on his heel and moved off, so fast that it was almost a run.

"Let him go," Pa said. "Let's get out of here."

It was a relief to get away. The last thing she remembered seeing was Mavis Boone, watching round eyed as they rode out of town. Liza could just imagine the gossip they had started that day.

The wagon ride back home was noticeably quiet, though to Liza the silence was without any sense of peace. Matthew sat with his shoulders hunched. He could have been a thousand miles away rather than sitting right next to her. His eyes kept going back to frown at the gold band that shone so brightly on his finger.

It wasn't until they were almost home that Liza finally broke the silence. "I don't believe it," she whispered. "We need to go down to Salem, look at whatever records they have there, question people. We should leave tomorrow."

"No," Matthew said. "We need to finish getting the crops into the barn. That cannot wait. The rains are going to start any day now."

"By tomorrow night, I'd say." Pa angled his head up to look at the dark clouds on the western ridge, tinged with red.

"I cannot stand wearing this bonnet a moment longer. It makes me feel trapped." Liza tugged impatiently at the ribbon and removed her bonnet, letting the wind ruffle her hair. "We have to do something about this woman."

"What would you suggest? She has evidence to back up her story." Matthew touched the ring on his finger, turning it so that the sunlight glinted off the gold band. "That fact alone makes her story all the more likely to be true."

Liza could not deny that, but she wanted to. "You've been on this claim for weeks now, and you said that miner could back up your statement that you were unmarried two months ago. So there's only a small window of time in which you could've married her. Someone, somewhere might remember you."

"This woman, Addy, has apparently been staying in Salem. Perhaps if I went down there after the harvest, I might find evidence to disprove her story."

On the surface, his words sounded positive. Even though she had wanted both of them to go, and he plainly intended to go on his own. But Liza could not shake off the feeling that he did not really believe what he was saying. It was as if he were trying to say what she wanted to hear. Her suspicions deepened into conviction. Liza had doubts about the woman's story, but clearly Matthew did not. She had to find a way to get him to listen to her.

She thought she might have a chance to talk with him privately later on, but after supper, when she suggested a walk, Matthew shook his head. "Tomorrow's going to be a long day."

"We could sit out on the bench, watch the stars come out," Liza offered.

"It's getting too cold at night to sit out there. No, I think I'll just turn in. Good night." And he was off to the barn without a glance in her direction. She had seen him in dark moods before, but he had never shut her out like this. This was bad. And she had a feeling it was going to get worse.

The next day, Matthew and Liza started at dawn. They only had one more field to harvest. Mr. Fitzpatrick hobbled outside and eyed the gathering clouds with a worried frown. "Work fast," was his advice. "I'll bring the wagon down at noon to start hauling the wheat back to the barn. We'll spread it out on the barn floor to dry."

There was a definite chill in the air this morning. Liza shivered as she and Matthew walked down to the wheat field. When they got to the field, Matthew leaned the scythe up against the fence and shrugged out of his jacket. "Here." He placed it around Liza's shoulders. "I'll be warm soon enough."

"Thank you," Liza said. "That's kind of you."

Matthew turned away. He could feel her looking at him, but he refused to meet her gaze. "It's not much," he said harshly. There was little he could do for her now. Addy had changed everything.

Mr. Fitzpatrick came down at noon, and Liza helped him load up the wagon with grain while Matthew kept cutting. He refused any offer of food, sweeping the scythe down the rows relentlessly. He worked so fast that Liza could barely keep up. When at last he finished and Mr. Fitzpatrick had driven the wagon off toward the barn one last time, he allowed himself a moment's satisfaction at a job well done. But that did not lighten his mood. This was an ending.

They were all quiet as they gathered around the supper table that evening. After supper, Liza got up. "Wait here," she told Matthew. She returned with a cake, which she placed on the table in front of him. "I made it last night. I had just enough of the apples and honey left," she said. "I'd planned this to be a celebration."

"We can still celebrate," her pa said. "The harvest is done."

"Oh, the cake isn't for that." She gave Matthew a curious look. "You don't remember, do you? Today is your birthday."

"I had forgotten." He gave a half laugh. "I still have a lot to remember. Thank you."

With an effort, he managed to eat the cake. It was perfectly baked, light and fluffy, and the apples were sweetly tart. But he might as well have been swallowing sawdust. He could no longer use the harvest as an excuse for staying here. It was tempting to put off talking to Liza, to savor their last moments of peace together. But he owed her the truth. He put down the fork. "That was delicious."

Liza nodded and got up to start stacking the dishes. Matthew stopped her. "Could I talk to you outside for a moment?"

Mr. Fitzpatrick said, "You two have done enough work for the day. I'll take care of cleaning up. Go out and have your talk."

Outside, the gray clouds were tinged with the last reds and golds of the setting sun. He could no longer see the peak of Mount Hood. The mountain was invisible, swathed in a mantle of rain clouds. It would be raining here soon enough. It was growing dark, but not as dark as the gloom he felt inside.

Liza led the way until they were out of earshot of the cabin. "I've been thinking. This marriage… that story the woman told…" She shook her head. "I don't believe it."

He looked down at Liza, this petite stranger he had apparently promised to marry on the Oregon Trail. She was a delicate little thing, dainty as a china doll, but with a stubborn streak as wide as the Mississippi. "How can you be so sure?" He was sure of nothing now, not even the ground under his feet. "We hadn't seen each other in almost a year."

"People don't change, not deep down. I trust you."

He clenched his fists. "Don't say that." He had let down everyone he had cared for. He had even let her down. This was just the pattern repeating itself again.

"No," she repeated. "I am not merely being stubborn. I know you better than you know yourself, apparently." She took his hand in hers. He stilled, watching her intently without moving. She went on, earnestly, "You will have to take my word for this. You are not a man who would break a promise."

He withdrew his hand, gently but decisively. "I don't know another way to interpret the evidence. It's a pretty convincing case. And I have no way of proving otherwise. For all I know, I could have married that woman."

"You're a fool if you believe that woman's story." She sighed. "But then, I'm a fool, as well. I honestly thought that this time, you might stay. One day, you are going to regain your memory and find out the truth. Until then, you need to have faith."

How could she be so trusting? It was growing dark, but that was nothing compared to the gloom he felt inside. "I have no faith. Not in myself."

"Well, then, I'll have faith enough for both of us."

She looked up at him, pretty as a prairie wild-flower, but he could see the effort it took her to smile. Her lips trembled. Her distress stirred up feelings he didn't dare contemplate. Not any longer. He took refuge behind a scowl. "It's getting late. You should go to bed."

He could not tell her tonight that he was leaving. It hurt too much to watch the pain he was causing. If she stayed, he was going to lose his resolve and take her in his arms. His defenses crumbled whenever she came near him. Tomorrow. He would tell her tomorrow.

He walked back to the barn, hands in his pockets. The loft was stuffed full of hay now, and most of the barn floor was taken up with wheat spread out to dry. He had folded up Liza's quilt just inside the door, with a bucket of water next to it for washing. The little kitten, Elijah, lay curled up in the middle of the quilt. He purred when Matthew stroked his head but did not open his eyes.

Matthew could not unfold the quilt without rousing the kitten. It was just as well. He felt too restless to sleep or even to sit still. The barn felt too stuffy. He needed air.

The clouds moving overhead were thicker now, but in the gaps between the clouds, the full moon shone so brightly that he could see to make his way down to the stream. He seated himself on a stump by the pool, where the moonlight reflected on the placid water.

When that woman, Addy, had slipped that ring on his finger, he'd had a clear flash of memory. He had been standing in the sunlight, holding his left hand up to look at the shining gold band . He had not seen Addy in that memory, but she was familiar. He had seen her before. And her story fit the facts with all the finality of a key turning in a lock. He should have known he would make a mess of his relationship with Liza. It was the pattern of his life, just as he had made a mess of things in the past, with his mother, with Vince.

He could not imagine why he would have offered another woman marriage. Possibly she had been caught in some compromising situation and honorable marriage was the only way to preserve her reputation. The details didn't matter. At least he had kept this one last promise he had made to Liza. He had finished the harvest, made sure she and her father were taken care of.

The irony of his situation was not lost on him. He had repudiated Liza back in the dry goods store, because he had felt as if he were being trapped by an unscrupulous woman who wanted to use him to further her own ends. And he had ended up in exactly the same position with another woman.

A voice in the back of his mind whispered that it might all still be some kind of elaborate scheme to keep him away from Liza and the claim. But based on his past history, the preponderance of evidence seemed to add up to the fact that, once again, he had let down someone he loved.

What really shook him was not Addy's story. It was the clear memory he had of putting on that wedding ring. He could picture it still. He had held the ring up, looking at the sunshine sparkling off the smooth gold. He remembered with perfect clarity the certainty he had felt. He had promised to wear that ring until the day he died. Regardless of whatever story Addy and Mr. Brown had cooked up between them, he really had gotten married.

He could not stay on the claim any longer. He could not bear to see Liza every day and know she would never be his wife. It was best to make a clean break of it. He couldn't ever come back here again. Liza would go on with her life, maybe marry someone else. He flinched away from that thought. No, he could not watch that happen. Once he left, he would not come back.

Finally, he got to his feet and headed back up the trail. As he started to cross the fields toward the house, he smelled smoke. A rosy glow flared up in the barn. Matthew began to run.

Chapter Thirteen

By the time Matthew reached the barn, the grain on the dirt floor had begun to catch fire. In the doorway, he collided with a shadowy figure running out. Not Mr. Fitzpatrick—a smaller man, of slight build. He grasped hold of the man to keep from falling over, and the other man swung around to get away. As he turned, Matthew caught sight of his face. He should have known.

Mr. Brown wrenched free and dashed off toward the road that led back to town. Matthew caught the faint sound of a horse stamping, bridle jingling as if the horse were agitated, then the sound of hoofbeats fading. There wasn't time to chase after him—smoke was beginning to seep under the barn door. He slipped inside, trying not to open the door any more than he had to.

In the light of the flames, he could see Mr. Fitzpatrick lying sprawled on the floor; blood trickled down his face. Even as Matthew started toward him, however, Mr. Fitzpatrick began to move, clambering to his feet and wiping blood away from his eyes. Grabbing the bucket of water, Matthew threw it on the flames. The water diminished the flames but did not extinguish the fire.

Mr. Fitzpatrick brushed past Matthew to the water trough outside. As he flung the barn door open, the inrush of air caused the flames to leap up again.

Matthew grabbed the heavy wedding quilt that was folded up by the door, swirling it out so that it was fully open when he flung it across the burning grain. Coughing, Mr. Fitzpatrick threw another bucket of water over the quilt. Clouds of steam mingled with the dark smoke, making it harder to see. The water dampened the fabric, and he and Matthew stomped down on the quilt again and again. Matthew grabbed the bucket and fetched more water while Mr. Fitzpatrick went on stamping until no more smoke came out from under the quilt. Even then, he continued to pour water until the quilt was waterlogged and rivulets of mud ran down the packed dirt floor.

"Right." Matthew took a deep breath. "I think it's out."

Mr. Fitzpatrick did not reply. He was bent over, coughing. When he could not stop coughing, Matthew grasped him by the arm. "Come on," he grunted, and headed for the door.

Liza woke suddenly. Lifting her head from the pillow, she listened intently. Had she dreamed the shouting? The fire in the fireplace had died down almost to nothing, but she climbed down the ladder and used one of the embers to light the lantern. She looked around. The cabin was quiet, but she had a bad feeling in the pit of her stomach. Lantern in hand, she went to the door and peered outside.

The barn was dark—no, not completely dark. The door was ajar. Inside, she could see orange sparks flaring to life. Not a lantern, not a candle. Wildfire. A breeze blew the scent of smoke up the path toward her, heady, overpoweringly strong. From the paddock, the horse neighed wildly.

She ran down the path as her heart thudded in a rhythm of terror. Matthew had been in the barn. Her mind fixated on that point. She could not think of what that might mean. She would not think of it.

By the time she reached the barn, clouds of gray billowed out, making it impossible to see inside clearly. The lantern was no help, so she set it down. "Matthew!" she called, coughing as the smoke entered her lungs. "Are you there?"

In response came an indignant meow. Even as she moved forward, a tiny bundle of fur streaked out of the darkness toward her. She caught the kitten up and held him close to her. He squirmed, still complaining, but she did not care. She held him close and choked out the words, "Oh, Elijah. Was he with you? Is he safe?"

The kitten wriggled his way into a more comfortable position and did not make any further complaints. Liza could feel how fast the little creature's heart was racing. It was beating no faster than her own heart.

Matthew came out of the smoke-filled doorway. He had his arm around Pa and helped him over to the stump to sit down. Half laughing, half sobbing, Liza threw her arms around Matthew as he straightened up. "I thought I'd lost you," was all she managed to get out.

She held onto him as if he were her lifeline and she were lost in a pathless wilderness. He was still breathing heavily. She could feel the rise and fall of his chest, and she became aware of how closely she was wrapped around him. She took a step back but still kept her hands on his chest, unwilling to part from him completely.

"No," he said. "That's too far away. I need you closer."

Very carefully, as if she were fragile as spun glass, he put his arms around her and pulled her close again. He was warm, his arms around her strong as if they could shut out the night and all the terror and fear she had felt. He still smelled of smoke, but she did not care. She laid her head down against his shoulder. She had never felt so safe or protected in her life. He bent his head so that his lips were by her ear, his breath warm against her neck. "Even if I never do this again, I need to hold you one last time." His arms tightened around her.

Liza closed her eyes, listening to the beat of his

heart, the rhythm of his breath as his chest rose and fell. His shirt was linen, thin from frequent washing, and smelled of wood smoke and sweat. She clung to him so tightly that there came a tiny mew of protest. Little Elijah popped his head up between them, urgently butting his head against Matthew's chest. Matthew sighed, letting go of Liza to take the kitten from her. He smiled down at her. "Well. I know I said the barn was toasty warm, but I didn't mean *this* warm."

She tried to smile but failed. "He knew you slept in the barn. Mr. Brown. I told him. He wanted to…" She couldn't complete the sentence.

Pa's coughing broke the moment. Matthew tilted his head, regarding him sitting on the stump. "You feeling all right? You don't look good."

Liza twisted around in fresh worry. "Pa? Can I get you some water?"

Pa nodded, still bent over. "I heard something outside. When I looked out, I saw someone light a lantern, so I went to see what was going on. Whoever he was, he was in the barn with his back to me. He was trying to toss the lantern up into the hayloft. I shouted at him, but when I went to stop him, he swung the lantern at me. Must have knocked me out for a moment; he was gone when I came to. I couldn't follow him—the grain was starting to smoke. I knew if a fire got started there'd be no stopping it."

"You're bleeding!" Liza smoothed back his hair to see the gash on his temple. "It looks horrible."

He patted her shoulder gently. "Not to worry, m'darling. Head wounds always bleed a lot."

"I'd feel better if we could get Doc Graham to look at you."

"It would be dawn before he got out here," Matthew pointed out. "We would do better to head into town as soon as it's light. We need to speak to the sheriff about this incident."

"It was Mr. Brown," Liza said.

"Of course it was." Pa coughed harder, bent over with his hands braced on his knees. He straightened, red faced and wheezing. "But we can't prove it."

"I can," Matthew said. "I saw him leaving the barn."

Pa started to get to his feet, then he swayed a bit and sat back down on the stump. "Maybe I'll just sit here for a bit."

"I think we all need a moment or two to recover from all the excitement," Matthew said wryly.

Liza looked at them both and was shaken with an almost physical pain at the intensity of the love coursing through her body. She opened her mouth to tell Matthew something of what she felt, but he had turned away to speak to Pa. "I think we'll have to risk leaving the claim unprotected. You need to see the doctor, and Liza needs to come with us."

"I suppose." Pa's mouth curved in a wry expression. "We can keep an eye on the barn for the next hour or two, make sure the fire's completely out, at any rate."

Liza held her tongue. There would be time enough for her to talk with Matthew later, after the doctor had had a chance to treat Pa.

They set out as soon as there was light enough in the eastern sky to see the ruts in the road. Matthew harnessed the horse while Liza milked the cows. Then she spread hay in the back of the wagon so Pa could lie down comfortably. It worried her that her independent pa did not protest that he could drive instead. A bad sign.

The trip to town seemed interminable. Liza sat huddled close to Matthew but turned around frequently to check on Pa. Pa rode with his eyes closed most of the way, but he did not seem rested. His face was flushed, and he could not stop the coughs that shook his body. Matthew drove carefully in the half-light, trying to avoid the worst of the ruts so he wouldn't jostle Pa. Liza appreciated his thoughtfulness, yet at the same time she had to suppress the urge to tell him to hurry.

Pa wasn't doing any better when they pulled up in front of Doc Graham's house. As Matthew helped him out of the wagon, Pa bent over almost double, his whole body racked with a fit of coughing. Liza put her hand on his shoulder. She had never felt so helpless.

Mrs. Graham came out onto the porch, evidently having heard their wagon rattle up. She checked the cut on Pa's head swiftly and nodded. "It's not too bad. Ben is away at the moment, but I can help."

Matthew put his arm around Pa and helped him inside the house. Mrs. Graham directed him to lay Pa down on a narrow bed in a back room. "Give me a moment to wash his wound and evaluate the damage to his lungs."

Liza went into the front room, followed by Matthew. The neat little room was comfortably furnished, with cane chairs and a sofa upholstered in fashionable plum-colored velvet. She sat down on the chair nearest the door. Matthew stood, his back against the wall, watching her. He said nothing. The only sound came from the clock on the mantelpiece, ticking away slices of eternity. Liza tried to form a prayer, but all she could think was, *Please. Please. Please let him live.*

It felt like years but was probably only a few minutes before Mrs. Graham came out into the room, wiping her hands on her apron. Liza sprang to her feet, and Matthew came to stand by her side. Mrs. Graham smiled at her. "I think he's going to be all right. The wound bled a lot, but the cut is superficial. The damage to his lungs is a bit more worrying. I don't think there's long-term damage, but I'd like him to rest here until Ben can see him. I don't think you need to worry."

"Oh, thank the Lord." The relief that filled her was so raw, it did not feel real.

"I've put a compress on his head, but I need to bandage the wound properly and then I'll see if I can help with that cough."

"Can I see him?" Liza asked hopefully.

"Yes, of course." Mrs. Graham looked at Matthew, who had not moved. Something in his expression seemed to convey a message to her, for she turned back to Liza. "Come back when you are ready." Then she left the room, shutting the door behind her.

Liza hung back, looking at Matthew. "You're not coming in?"

"I'm going now," Matthew said.

"Going?" She said slowly. "You mean to Frank, to have him arrest Mr. Brown."

Matthew met her eyes. He did not reply. In that moment, she knew. "No," she said. "Don't go. Not now. Wait until Pa is better. We need to work together to find out what this Addy woman is really up to."

He shook his head. "A clean break is best," he said. "I'll go to the sheriff first, tell him about Mr. Brown. I can bear witness, say that I saw him with my own eyes. That's enough to get him put in jail. He won't bother you any longer."

"If you stay, maybe we can find a way to—"

"I can't," he whispered. "I can't marry you. Addy has seen to that. For whatever reason, I remember putting that ring on my finger. And I can't be close to you, see you every day and not touch you ever again." He raised his hand, gently cupped her cheek. "Just this one last time." Then he turned away. He did not look back.

There was nothing she could do to stop him. She had never felt so helpless. Blinking back tears, she clenched her hand around the door frame and watched his back until he turned the corner that led to the jail. Then she went inside and closed the door. Matthew was gone. She had always known he was going to leave. He had left her before, after all. And she knew she could survive without him. She just had forgotten how cold the world could feel when you had been abandoned.

Dawson wasn't in his little office by the jail. To Matthew's surprise, Petey was there, stretched out on the narrow cot in the cell. The miner was fast asleep, snoring faintly.

"I think he's starting to see it as his new home," Dawson said from the doorway. He hung his battered old hat on the hook by the door.

"Mr. Brown tried to burn down the Fitzpatricks' barn last night." Matthew wasted no time. "He injured Liza's pa. The man's at Doc Graham's now."

"That so." Dawson shrugged off his weather-beaten jacket.

Dawson went through a doorway in the back that Matthew hadn't noticed before. He caught a glimpse of a bed and a dresser, the sheriff's personal room, evidently.

"I am going to go over to the hotel to confront him," Matthew added, raising his voice to carry to the next room.

Dawson came out again, wearing his Sunday best coat and carrying a spruced-up hat.

"Well?" Matthew prompted. "I saw Mr. Brown running out of the barn after it had caught fire. There's no question that he set it. Liza will attest that she told him I sleep in the barn loft. That's not only arson, it's attempted murder."

"Yep," Dawson said placidly. He stood in front of the little window, looking at his reflection as he straightened his tie. "Just came back from a trip over to the hotel, as a matter of fact. Seems our Mr. Brown done skipped out this morning, cleared out his room and left without paying his bill. Manager's mad as a wet hen, wanted to file a complaint. But I can't arrest the man until I find him. If I do."

"You think he's hiding up at the Baron's mansion?" Matthew began to understand. The Baron lived in a grand new house set up on the bluff overlooking Oregon City. Lots of room to hide a fugitive, if the Baron were so inclined.

Dawson shook his head. "I doubt it. I can't see the Baron putting up with that kind of nonsense, not now that he's going in for politics. The man's not a fool. But he might know where Mr. Brown went. I better go and make sure."

The sheriff picked up his hat and turned for the door.

"One more thing," Matthew said.

Dawson stopped, his head cocked to one side and his eyes fixed on Matthew.

A deep breath. "I'm leaving town."

Dawson said nothing.

"So I'm hoping you'll keep an eye on—that is, if she needs any help—not that she isn't perfectly competent, but everyone can use a friend at times—oh, you know what I'm trying to say," Matthew snarled.

"Ay, I reckon I do." Dawson nodded. "I'm not going to stop being her friend just 'cause she's in love with a fool."

"What do you expect me to do? I have to clean up this mess with that Addy woman. I am not going to involve Liza in that!"

Dawson opened his mouth to speak and then stopped as a grizzled older man entered. "I heard my friend Petey's been causing trouble again." Wearing disreputable-looking clothing and a red bandanna, the man had the ingrained dirt that Matthew had come to recognize from his time in the mines. He stopped dead when he caught sight of Matthew. "Well, I'll be—Dean! What are you doing here? If that don't beat all. Here I've been acting as postman for you, and you right here."

Matthew narrowed his eyes. "Do I know—" he stopped. "Carter," he said slowly. "That's your name. I remember. You helped Vince when he first came to Dutch Flat. What do you mean, acting postman for me?"

The man looked embarrassed. "When I left Dutch Flat, I know I told you I meant to come straight up here. But I heard a rumor about gold in Jacksonville, and then I got sick, and, well, you got here before I did." The man put down his knapsack and knelt to rummage around in it. "I still got the letter you gave me. Ah, here it is." The man handed Matthew an envelope. It was dirty and crumpled, but he could still read the direction written on it.

"What is it?" Dawson asked.

"I sent a letter to Liza, it seems." The elegant, slanted copperplate handwriting looked vaguely familiar. He weighed the letter in his hand. Would it be snooping to read a letter from himself? He didn't have time, in any case. "Thanks, Carter. I'll send this letter on to its recipient."

Carter slung the knapsack over his shoulder again. He looked at the sleeping figure in the cell. "Guess I'll let Petey sleep his fill. I'll come back later."

"Wait." Matthew held up his hand. "A moment. How did you get here?"

"There's a boat." Carter blinked at him, seemingly surprised by the question. "I caught it in Salem."

"That's what I thought." Matthew nodded his thanks. The miner moved off, and he turned to Dawson. "This is my chance to get to Salem."

"Now?" Dawson frowned.

"Mr. Brown's gone," Matthew said impatiently. "But if he forged some kind of paperwork down in Salem about me marrying that woman, I need to be the one to put a stop to it. A marriage has to have witnesses to be legal. If I can't remember *not* marrying her, I need to prove that I'm not the man the witnesses saw during the ceremony—if there really was a ceremony at all. No one else can do that for me." *And I need to find out whom I really did marry, what led me to put that wedding ring on and vow never to take it off again.*

That was the problem, really. He had put that ring on his hand. The truth twisted inside him like a knife to his gut. He had made a lifelong promise to another woman. He could never return to Liza. He had already said goodbye. This was his chance to make the break as cleanly as possible.

Dawson sighed. "Canemah is a whole mile upriver. The *Multnomah* only stays there long enough to refill the wood lot for the boiler. Then it's off to Salem again. If you want to catch the boat before it leaves, you'll need a horse. My Beau is the fastest thing round these parts. Come on." He headed toward the door.

Matthew followed. "You'll loan me your horse?"

"The Fitzpatricks' nag is too old, too slow. My Beau is fresh. He'll get you there in time." Behind the jail, the black gelding was housed in a little stable. Dawson swapped out its halter for the bridle that was hanging on the post. Then he hoisted up the saddle, eyeing Matthew's legs. "You might want to lengthen the stirrups a bit. Leave Beau at Taylor's livery stables. They'll take care of him till I can send a boy out to fetch him."

"And if you do track down Mr. Brown, you are going to arrest him, right?" Matthew swung himself up into the saddle with a creaking of leather.

"That's one thing we can agree on." Dawson nodded. "At this rate, I might come to have some respect for you after all."

"I'm not sure you want to go that far," Matthew warned. Underneath that mustache, he thought he detected the slightest upward quirk of a smile. He leaned down and handed the envelope to Dawson. Here he was, leaving Liza with another note—and he did not even know what it contained. Probably an explanation of why he had been delayed in California. He wished he had time to read it himself. "Give this to Liza from me. Tell her…" He hesitated, then shook his head. "Look after Liza."

"You'll be back. You're as stubborn as she is." Everyone else seemed to have faith in him. Given his past history of always being too late, he wasn't sure they should trust him so much. He gathered up the reins and touched his heels to the horse's flanks, heading around Dawson toward the open street.

Liza came into the back room, where Mrs. Graham was bandaging up Pa's head. "What can I do?"

Mrs. Graham smiled at her, as if she understood how important it was for Liza to have something to do. "The kitchen is at the end of the hall. If you could build up the fire and get the kettle boiling, that would be a great help. Ben usually recommends herbs soaked in steaming-hot water."

By the time Liza came back into the room with the kettle, Mrs. Graham was helping Pa make his way over to the table, where a large basin sat. She took the kettle from Liza, poured the hot water into the basin and scattered the herbs into the water. "Here." She handed Pa a towel. "Place this over your head, then lean forward over the basin. Take deep breaths." To Liza, she said softly, "It might be better if you were to wait in the other room, dear. He keeps trying to speak. There's something he wants to tell you, but it would be best if he rested until after the treatment."

Liza nodded and slipped out into the other room. It was too empty now without Matthew. She could not stand the thought of sitting there listening to that clock. She would just step outside for a moment to get a breath of air.

That was the plan, until she saw Frank Dawson coming down the plank sidewalk toward her. She had never seen him look so solemn and forbidding. Matthew was nowhere in sight.

She waited, not moving, barely breathing, until Frank stopped in front of her. The look of pity in his eyes was as bad as a blow. Worse. She whispered, "Is he gone already?" Somewhere in the back of her mind, she had thought he might change his mind, that something would delay him until she'd had a chance to persuade him, until she could have done *some*thing to stop him. He'd left her. Again.

"He had to leave right away if he was going to catch the boat for Salem." Frank hesitated and then drew something out from his jacket. He placed an envelope in her hand. "He left you a note. He'd sent it when he was down in California. We don't always get mail reliably, you know that."

She did not want to think about Matthew leaving. That wound was too fresh. There wasn't time now, anyway. "Did he tell you about Mr. Brown setting the fire?"

"Yep. I was on my way to see the Baron, find out where Brown's gotten to."

"I'll go with you." If Liza didn't do *something*, she was going to scream.

"You can't," Frank said with his usual rigid logic. "You have to stay with your pa. Dean said he got hurt."

Liza closed her eyes. Pa needed her. She could not go off without seeing how he was. "Where— where was Matthew going to catch the boat?" She didn't know why she even asked. It wasn't as if she could go off to catch the boat with him.

"He went up toward Canemah. But he's probably gone by now." Frank paused, watching her. "Are you going to be all right? I have to go see the Baron now. I should have gone already, but I wanted you to get that letter. Dean seemed to think it pretty important."

"Thank you," she whispered. Frank hesitated, as if expecting her to say more, then he gave a jerky nod and moved on, heading for the trail that led up the hill.

Liza waited until he had turned the corner, then she moved. She couldn't go far—she would stay within earshot—but she needed to see for herself.

She crossed the road to the alley between the livery stables and the blacksmith's shop. That led her to the edge of town, giving her a view of the river to the south. She thought she caught a glimpse of the white steamboat disappearing around the bend, but that might have been her imagination. It was hard to be sure when tears blurred her vision. She heard the distant *toot-toot* of a steamboat's whistle, and there was a faint whiff of black smoke that might have come from a smokestack. He was gone.

They always left. It was safer to be on her own, relying on no one but herself. That way, she couldn't get hurt.

She looked down at the letter still clenched in her hand. With fingers suddenly stiff from tension, she broke the seal and scanned the page. She could not seem to stop the tears from flowing. It made reading difficult. Words and phrases leaped out at her. "Missing you… I think of you every day… We've found a vein. It looks promising. I might have to stay a little longer to see if it pans out, but I promise you that I will be at your side within the year… I saved the first nugget of gold that I found. I keep it hidden

in the toe of my boot so it won't get lost or stolen...
As soon as I find someone who can do the work, I
will have him make the nugget into a pair of wedding rings. I will wear my ring on my finger as soon
as I have it made. As far as I am concerned, we are
already married. My heart is in your keeping."

She refolded the letter and looked upriver once
more. In the distance, she heard the faint sound of
the steamboat's whistle again, *toot-toot*. It sounded
like a funeral bell tolling a death knell.

Chapter Fourteen

If you leave this time, don't expect me to wait for you.

Matthew kept hearing those words in his head as he rode south along the bluff. Dark clouds were blowing in from the west, bringing with them a smattering of raindrops but no storm, not just yet. The weather only gave him more reason to hurry.

Even if he found some loophole that invalidated his marriage to Addy, he had married someone. And if he *had* made some promises to Addy, he was responsible for her welfare. His thoughts chased each other. He did not know what was true any longer. He was more lost than when he'd woken up in the dry goods store.

Canemah turned out to be a tiny village upriver from the waterfall, situated where the current had carved a little harbor out of the riverbank. Matthew made sure the gelding had a good drink at the watering trough before tying him to a post by the livery stables. There were few boats in the river, apart from the steamboat. The *Multnomah* was moored at a dock that extended out into the river. It looked incongruous to see such a new, prosperous-looking side-wheeler on a western river. A steamboat belonged on the Mississippi or some river back east.

They had evidently finished loading up the wood for the boiler. Wisps of black smoke escaped from the long black smokestack, and passengers were lining up to board. He had gotten there just in time. Off to one side, a little boy, clearly bored with all the standing around that the adults were doing, was playing by himself along the riverbank, poking at the water with a stick. His mother, a tired-looking young woman, called him back and he reluctantly came, flourishing his stick as if it were a sword. Matthew got into line behind them. The boy looked over his shoulder at Matthew and then looked away again, shy. His mother kept hold of him with one hand while she spoke to a woman on her other side about the trip to Salem.

Don't expect me to wait for you.

He could not get Liza's words out of his mind. He didn't want to leave her hating him. When she'd said those words to him, she'd been upset. She had been angry with him for leaving her on the Trail, and she had hoarded her resentment like a miser's gold. She needed to let go of that anger before she could go on with her life.

Lord, this is beyond my control, but nothing is

beyond You. You have enough love to forgive me for my sins. Help Liza to do the same.

He could do nothing more to help her. He would have to get used to that fact. He was never going to see her again.

Liza found Pa resting on a narrow bed, lying back with his eyes closed. He looked unnaturally pale, but he evidently heard her come in, for he opened his eyes and smiled at her. She grasped his rough, callused hand in both of hers. "Oh, Pa!" She put his hand up against her cheek and closed her eyes to keep the tears from flowing. He was going to be fine. She would not distress him by crying.

"Go ahead and cry, Lizzy darlin'."

"No." She got the word out between gritted teeth.

"Stubborn girl," he wheezed. "You must get that from me. Sure, and you didn't get it from your mother." His Irish accent was more pronounced than usual, a clear sign he was more upset than he was trying to let on.

"You shouldn't talk. Mrs. Graham said—"

"I have to speak. There are things that need saying between you and me."

"Pa…"

"I need to tell you this. In case anything happens to me." He grasped her hand, held it. "I got the claim for you. It's for your future. Women can't claim land in this territory, but they can inherit it. You decide what should be done with it. You can sell it and get enough money to live where you will, set up in a line of work, perhaps, if you don't want to marry. It gives you choices in what to do with your life."

It is everything I thought I wanted. And nothing I truly need. I see that now. She took his hand, pressed it against her cheek. She felt too full of emotion for any more words. He lay back with his eyes closed. Eventually, his breathing relaxed into a deep sleep.

She sat there in silence until a knock came at the door. Mrs. Graham came in. To Liza, she said softly, "I think it would be all right to let your father rest for a while. There are some visitors here for you."

Liza shut the door behind her as she stepped into the sitting room. Granny Whitlow and Mavis Boone were sitting on the stiff horsehair sofa. Granny had the seat nearer the stove, of course, and was looking her usual calm, cynical self. Mavis sat bolt upright. Mrs. Graham seated herself on the cane chair in the corner. They all looked at Liza.

She came forward and sat in the chair farthest from the fireplace. The concerted gazes of all three women were a bit unnerving. To counteract this, Liza took her time spreading out her skirt, taking care to fold her hands gracefully in her lap. They had come for the latest gossip, she supposed. Fair enough. There was something she needed from them, as well.

She took a deep breath. "Last night Mr. Brown set fire to my barn in an attempt to murder the man who was helping us get in the harvest. I think he was also behind that woman who claimed to be married to Matth—to Mr. Dean."

Mavis's eyes grew round. Liza had thought at first that this was merely her normal reaction to a piece of scandalous gossip. But then Mavis said, "I never did believe that woman's story."

"I beg your pardon?"

For once, Mavis didn't look excited over the prospect of delicious gossip. Her eyes were solemn. "I don't believe that Mr. Dean would have come all this way only to turn aside at the last minute and marry someone else. He came here for you."

Liza lifted her eyebrows. "I thought you didn't believe in romantic fairy tales."

"Well, I've changed my mind," Mavis said defiantly. "I've seen the way he looks at you. That's true love."

"The girl's right," Granny agreed. "Pay no mind to that fancy woman."

Mrs. Graham said softly, "She must be in dreadful straits to resort to such lies."

"And I think you're right about someone pushing her to make this claim." Granny leaned forward, directing her attention to Mavis and Mrs. Graham. "Between the three of us, we know pretty much everything that goes on in this town. It should be easy enough to find out what she is up to."

It was heartening to find that these women supported Matthew. Liza had been so focused on their penchant for gossip, she should have realized that it was accompanied by loyalty. The townspeople had accepted Matthew as one of their own. Well, Granny Whitlow, Mrs. Graham and Mavis Boone had, but they were enough of a force that Liza reckoned the rest of the town would follow suit. It probably wouldn't be enough to sway the Baron, but it might be enough to create a wedge of doubt in the eyes of other citizens.

"I need to find out why she would claim that she was married to Matthew. The difficulty is finding proof that she was lying. There must be some evidence. I find it hard to believe that she just popped up in Oregon City and no one knows anything about her."

Mrs. Graham said, "I think that she must have been in town for a little while. That bonnet she was wearing the other day was trimmed in that black braid the McKays just got into the store recently. She couldn't have gotten that down in Salem, and the trim looked new, as if she had updated her bonnet quite recently."

"Yes!" Liza stared at the other woman. "I'd never seen her before, but I knew that looked familiar. Mr. Brown bought that trim from me the last time I minded the store. Oh, the snake! He must have known her all that time."

"It's not much proof," Granny said doubtfully.

"It's a start," Liza said. "If only I knew where she was now."

"She's staying at the hotel," Mavis put in. "Up on the second floor, in a room that has a lovely view of the falls." The other women all looked at her, and she blushed slightly. "I...er, got to talking with one of the maids at the hotel. She told me."

"What is she like?" Liza asked. "When she's not trying to bamboozle defenseless men into marrying her, that is."

Mavis tilted her hand from side to side. "She keeps to herself, doesn't go out much or speak to anyone. I don't think she's a bad person, from how the maid described her. But she's definitely afraid of something."

"If there's something she is afraid of, then maybe I have a chance. There has to be some way to persuade her to help me. I need to make her an ally, but I do not know how."

"Why does she want your man?" Granny made a little tch'ing noise with her tongue.

"Mr. Dean is a fine-looking man," Mavis said. She blushed when Granny gave her a look but stood her ground. "Well, it's true."

"Yes, but why *him*?" Granny persisted. "If Mr. Brown isn't bribing her to help him, then there must be something about this man that suits her. Looks or no, there's plenty of other men around if all she wanted was a husband. No need to go pinching one that was already claimed."

"What I think," Mrs. Graham said, in her soft voice, "is that the best way to answer that question is just to ask her."

"That sounds almost too simple," Liza said.

"That doesn't mean it wouldn't work. You should go now. Your father is sleeping peacefully. There's nothing more you can do for him at the moment. You'll be better off doing something."

Liza stood up. "It's worth a try. Mavis, come show me which room this woman is staying in."

When Liza knocked on the hotel room door, Addy answered it immediately. She looked different—faded, somehow. Her face was pale, and her hair was slipping out of its net. There were dark circles under her eyes. She avoided meeting Liza's gaze and gestured her to enter the room.

"I was thinking of coming to see you," she said in a low voice. "The maid told me that your father was at the doctor's. I should have expected that you would come by. Come in." Liza stepped into a small room, very plain, with only a small bed and a table with two chairs. On the bed, a satchel lay open. A half-folded dress was draped across the bed. A wedding portrait had been tossed carelessly on top of it—Addy and some dark-haired man with a mustache.

Now that she was here, Liza found it hard to start the conversation. She looked at the picture. "I forgot. You said that you were a widow."

"I'm not." Addy avoided looking directly at Liza. "My husband went off to search for gold. He didn't want me to come. Last I heard, he'd taken up with some other woman. That was some months ago, and I haven't heard from him since. He doesn't want me." Liza merely stared at her, and Addy added, "That's why I did it, you see. I was desperate."

Liza blinked. She had come prepared to argue or plead with Addy, and here the other woman was openly confessing what she had done. She wanted more details, but there were other things she needed to know first. "Where is Mr. Brown?"

"He went off to see the Baron late last night. He hasn't come back." Addy crossed to the table and sat down. She gestured for Liza to take the other seat. "I told him that I won't put up with this anymore. I never planned for anyone to get hurt."

Gingerly, Liza sank down into the chair. It was a plain rush-woven seat. She gripped its edge. It was rough and hard, and she found it a comfort to have something solid to hold on to. It was as if she were taking part in a play where all the roles had changed at the last minute. "You—you were in on this with Mr. Brown, in his plan? Was this scheme his idea, or the Baron's?"

"I don't know the Baron. I've only heard about him. I know Alfred. Or at least," she added bitterly, "I thought I knew him."

Liza looked at her sharply. "Alfred? You—and Mr. Brown—were—"

She could not even complete the sentence, but Addy nodded. "I was a fool. I know. I thought that I could trust Alfred because I knew so much about his dealings. But you can't trust any man, really."

I trusted Matthew with all my heart. I still do, even now he's left me. Liza shook her head as though to clear it. She had to focus. She said simply, "Why did you do it?"

"I don't expect you to understand," Addy began. "But I honestly did not see what else I could do. I

came up here from California with my husband—
that part was true. He was a miner, and he heard
there was gold up in Jacksonville. When he couldn't
find a way to strike it rich quick, he lit out one night.
That was months ago." Addy gripped her handkerchief so hard that her nails broke through the thin
fabric. She relaxed with a visible effort. "I tried
selling my jewelry at first. I didn't have much—
my wedding ring, my grandmother's earrings... I
thought about selling a lot more than that. I was at a
low point when I met Alfred." She raised her eyes to
meet Liza's for a moment and then dropped her gaze
back to the handkerchief in her lap. "I know what
you think of Alfred. But if he hadn't helped me, I
wouldn't have survived. I was grateful. I wanted to
help him. I figured I owed it to him."

Liza wasn't sure she even wanted to ask for any
details about Addy's relationship with Mr. Brown.
"So you agreed to pose as the grieving wife of a
man you'd never met."

Addy shook her head. "That came later. Alfred
brought me up to Oregon City. He *said* it was to
see if I could get work here. At least, that's what he
said when I was down in Salem. When I got here,
he...well, he wanted me to stay in my room here at
the hotel and not go out. I only saw him. He found
that...convenient. I was waiting here when he came
in a tearing hurry one night. He needed me to come
out and help him lure a man into an alley. Some man
he'd met in the street, asking for directions to see
you. He'd given him misleading directions, to buy

time. There was some plan to kidnap the man, take him downriver to Astoria."

"Matthew."

Addy nodded. "Alfred said all they were going to do was put a bag over his head and send him on a boat down to Astoria. I don't think they expected him to fight back as hard as he did. There wasn't supposed to be any violence," she added virtuously.

Liza wasn't sure how to reconcile that with the cuts on Matthew's forehead and jaw, but she let it pass. There was something else she wanted to know. "How did he end up in the river?"

"Apparently, he fell during the fight. I don't know. I didn't see that part. I'd gone back to the hotel. I think they all thought he had drowned in the river. I didn't know he'd even been hurt until the next day, when Alfred said he'd showed up at the dry goods store. When he found out that you were planning to have him stay on the claim, he was furious. He said we had to come up with a new plan."

She twisted the handkerchief in her lap, avoiding Liza's gaze. "Alfred figured that he could forge a license and pass me off as your man's wife. By that time, I'd given up hope of hearing from my own husband. I don't think he'd know where to look for me even if he did bother. I doubt he ever would. No man would want to marry me up here. Not if they knew I had a husband probably still living, out there somewhere. Or if they knew..." Her voice trailed off, and she put her hand on her stomach for a moment, a brief protective gesture. "I didn't really see that I had all that much choice."

Liza sat there looking at the woman for a long moment. "So why are you telling me all this now?"

"Because Alfred came to see me late last night," Addy said. Her voice was so low Liza barely caught the words. "He said—he said that there had been an accident, that a man had been hurt and that there had been witnesses. Alfred thought he might have killed him."

"He was trying to kill Matthew," Liza said flatly.

"I didn't know!" Addy practically wailed the words. "I never meant anyone to get hurt, never. I finally told Alfred I would not provide him with an alibi for last night. Then he left me and went to see the Baron. That's all I know." She wiped her eyes with the handkerchief.

Liza regarded the weeping woman. Despite all the things that Addy had done, she felt a pang of concern. She had been abandoned, too. "So…what are you going to do now?"

"I don't know what to do." Addy hunched her shoulders, looking down at the handkerchief in her hands. She twisted the wedding band off her finger and gave it to Liza. "I don't know what happened to the other things Alfred took from your man, but this belongs to you, seemingly. I'm sorry I ever joined in with Alfred's scheme. I'd love to not be dependent on a man. But a single woman out here can't claim land. Anyway, I'm better off in a town."

"Are you still going to tell people you are married to him?"

"No. I just want to make a fresh start somewhere."

"We'll have to find you some kind of work."

"I could get work as a seamstress, if there's need of that up here." Addy fingered the braided trim on her bonnet. "Albert used to bring me presents like this trim, so I'd have something to do with my time. I could make a living that way, maybe."

Liza reached out and clasped Addy's hands. "The Baron can help you and *should*. After all, you were working for Mr. Brown, and he was working for the Baron, so in a sense you were his employee."

"The Baron?" Addy's eyes widened. "You would dare to go to him? Alfred said he has a fearsome temper."

"Oh, yes, I would dare." Liza thought of Pa, lying in the wagon and coughing. "In fact, I think we should go right now. Hopefully, Mr. Brown will be there, too. I think it's time for both of them to find out that I have a fearsome temper, as well."

She started to get up, but Addy put her hand on her arm. "Wait. I need to know. Can you forgive me?"

Liza hesitated, looking at the anxiety on the woman's face. She had spent the past year trying to protect herself from getting hurt, to steel herself against Matthew leaving her just as her pa had. Using a wall of resentment to stop herself from getting hurt. It couldn't be done. She was not going to travel down that road with Addy.

"Yes," she said slowly. "You were abandoned and in a desperate spot. I forgive you."

Addy tightened her grip on Liza's arm, a brief squeeze, then let go. She let out her breath in a rush, looking relieved. Liza felt lighter herself, letting go of the dark thoughts, the last of the anger she had held onto all this time. The only thing driving her now was her determination to resolve this mess. If that meant going to the Baron, so be it.

As Matthew waited to board the steamboat, a man came out of the goods shed. He was deep in conversation with a gray-haired man with a neatly trimmed beard, who wore a captain's uniform. They shook hands and then the captain turned toward the *Multnomah*. As the other man headed in Matthew's direction, he recognized Doc Graham. "Doctor!"

The doctor peered at him over his spectacles. "Ah, Dean." He stopped upon taking a closer look at Matthew's expression. "Is something the matter?"

In a few terse words, Matthew explained about Liza's father and Mr. Brown's abortive attempt to burn down the barn. The doctor's normally cherubic face looked positively grim by the time Matthew finished. "I suspected Mr. Brown was up to something, but I wasn't sure. He wanted me to declare you mentally unfit, get you locked up, but there was no way he could prove anything of the sort. It galled him when the Baron seemed so impressed by your knowledge of the law and that Liza was so attached to you. I should have warned you more clearly that he was going to try something to get you out of the way. But I was afraid that he might harm my family. I was wrong to keep silent. Cowardice only encourages a bully."

"At least Mr. Brown seems to have cleared out of Oregon City. Probably panicked."

The doctor nodded. "The Baron would never put up with the embarrassment of one of his men being caught behaving like the lowest form of criminal. Is Mr. Fitzpatrick badly injured?"

"Your wife didn't seem to think so, but I know Liza would feel better if you could examine her father as soon as you can. Do you have transportation back to Oregon City?"

"No, I was hoping I could catch a ride with one of the other passengers, but I was delayed with the captain and they've all gone on. I shall have to rely on Shanks's mare," he said a bit sadly.

"It's over a mile. A long walk when it's starting to rain," Matthew said. "You could do me a favor by returning Dawson's gelding to him. I left the horse tied up outside the livery stables."

The doctor thanked him profusely, and Matthew watched him ride off. The passengers still had not gotten leave to board the steamboat. Apparently the captain had to load the mail and supplies for the up-river traffic before he would take on passengers.

Ahead of Matthew, the little boy jiggled from side to side. His mother rebuked him, gently, and the boy settled down to sulk quietly by her side. Matthew grimaced. He could remember the frustration of always having to be a model of deportment when you were bursting with energy. Adults never could understand that. Well, except for his mother, and even she had expected him to act like a little adult at times. She had always seemed so tired, and just a bit sad, so he had tried hard to please her as best he could.

Another memory had returned, it seemed. They were fitting back into his mind so easily that he hardly noticed the gaps—except for the past few months before he came here, and his flight from Liza at Fort Hall. Eventually, he would recover all his memories, he felt sure of it. There was nothing he could achieve by fretting, but this missing part of himself was one more brick in the wall of frustration that blocked him from achieving his goals.

Every instinct he possessed was shouting at him to turn around and go back. There was no telling what Liza would do. She was brave enough to take on the Baron himself. He had seen how fierce she could be when her protective instincts were aroused.

If she were going to go up against the Baron, she would need Matthew by her side. Where he belonged. Where he had no right to be. He had forfeited any claim when he made a commitment to another woman.

The rain began to fall in earnest as the line of passengers finally shuffled forward up the dock. Crossing the plank to the boat felt like severing the last tie that held him to Liza. He clenched his hands into fists, but he kept moving forward, one foot in front of the other, until he stood on the deck.

The other passengers hurried onto the sheltered portico of the main deck to get out of the rain, all except the little boy, who hung back to watch the sailors moving about on the deck, readying the steamboat for its departure. Matthew could see the smokestack far above beginning to belch black smoke as the men in the boiler room stoked the furnace. On deck, the sailors began to cast off the mooring ropes. One sailor tossed back the rope that moored the stern rope, behind the paddle box. The lower end of the boat began to swing free as the current tugged it into the middle of the river. The little boy, caught off balance as he stood by the bow, slipped on the rain-slick deck. Wildly, he waved his arms around in an attempt to regain his footing. Then, with a wail, he fell. His cry was abruptly cut off as he entered the water. His mother shrieked. The sailor cursed. From behind him, Matthew could hear the captain bellowing orders. But he paid no attention to any of this. He dived headfirst after the boy into the river.

It was like diving into a coal cellar filled with ice water. He could not see, and the cold shocked through his system.

He remembered.

Coming into Oregon City just as evening was starting to fall. Asking for directions to where Liza was staying. The woman in the alley, calling for his help. The fight. Black water closing over his head. Panicking, flailing his arms and legs around.

His outstretched hand made contact with an arm, then a small hand. He grabbed hold of it and held on tightly. But he did not know which way was up, what direction to swim toward the air his lungs were suddenly begging for. He was completely disoriented.

Struggling until he found firm ground underfoot. Staggering up a dark street, blood in his eyes, heading toward a door with light behind it. Another woman, this one standing in the middle of a room with lantern light transforming her hair into a golden aureole around her. She seemed like an anchor, someone he could hold on to in this whirlpool of confusion. Instinctively he reached out to her just as the darkness claimed him again.

His head broke the water. He gulped in air, raising the child's head up above the surface. The boy was trying to sob and gasping for air at the same time. He clung to Matthew's neck, half choking him. Matthew blinked water out of his eyes. Someone had thrown him a rope. He grabbed at it and was swiftly towed to the steamboat, where eager hands pulled him up onto the deck.

The air on the deck was, if possible, even more freezing than the water. The breeze cut through Matthew's sodden clothing like a thousand knives. The boy's mother swooped down on her child, carrying him off to the warmer regions inside while babbling incoherent thanks to Matthew. Matthew wrapped his arms about himself, hugging himself in an attempt to get warm. He could not stop shaking. The captain threw a blanket over Matthew's shoulders. "Well done," he said, giving him a firm handshake. "Come inside the cabin, man. We need to get you warmed up."

"Thank you," Matthew gasped. "But I don't think I'll need to make this trip after all. I need to get off this ship. Now. I have to go back."

At last, he could remember. He knew where he had been and what he had been doing all this past year—and what he hadn't done. He could testify in court, if necessary, that he knew where he'd seen that woman before. And it hadn't been at a wedding.

Chapter Fifteen

They couldn't just let him leave, of course. First he had to be thanked by the half-hysterical mother, the captain and most of the passengers and crew. The captain backed the boat up to the dock long enough for Matthew to disembark, and he insisted that the goods shed superintendent see that Matthew got a change of clothes and some hot coffee. He had to admit that he needed both. It had stopped raining, for the moment, but he was still shaking from the effects of the cold water. The hot coffee was marvelously warming as he drank it. Nevertheless, he fretted over the delay. He had a sense that he didn't have much time to waste. He had finally regained the missing pieces of his memory.

He remembered that night in Fort Hall, when he had left Liza. She had been laughing when she made the remark about having six children, but that night he could not sleep. He'd taken a walk to try to sort things out in his own mind. All he could think of was the memory of his mother, worn down by work and worry into an early grave. He paced through the night, trying to think of a solution. What if something happened to him? Liza would be in the same position as his mother. And then he had come across the young men.

They had been sitting around a campfire, eating a predawn breakfast of cold bread and salt pork, talking about how they were all going to strike it rich in the goldfields in California. Matthew had taken it for no more than the usual round of idle boasting at first. Then one of the men had taken a piece of paper out of an inner pocket and showed it to him. It turned out to be a much-folded page from a newspaper in Sacramento. "My cousin out in Hangtown sent it to me," the man explained. He pointed to an etching of an enormous nugget of gold that had been found at Sutter's Mill. "This fellow pulled five thousand dollars' worth of gold right out of the ground," the man had said, folding the newspaper carefully back up and tucking it away again. "His grandchildren's grandchildren will be bragging about him a hundred years from now. That's what's waiting for me in California. Fame and fortune for anyone brave enough to grab for it."

Matthew had no use for fame, but with Liza wanting a passel of children, he might well need a fortune or two.

The group of young men were leaving at first light to head out on the California trail. They wouldn't wait for Matthew to take his leave of Liza.

They were traveling on horseback, moving fast. He didn't know when the next group heading for California would come by, but they would more than likely be a wagon train, drawn by slow and ponderous oxen. That was part of the appeal of this group; they would get to California weeks before any wagon train, probably even before Liza had arrived in Oregon. He could pick up his share of gold and be off to Oregon before she had time to miss him.

It was crazy, a reckless adventure. But it could save Liza. There was no way he was going to watch his bride suffer through a lifetime of working herself into an early grave, the way his poor mother had done. He was not going to let that happen. The sky behind the eastern mountains had been growing perceptibly lighter. He could start to see the landscape around him, beyond the dying fire. The young men started packing up their belongings.

Even from the distance of a year's time, he remembered the absolute conviction he had felt that it was worth any sacrifice if he could save Liza from suffering. That was what had decided him. Without stopping to think, he had gone to speak to her.

She was traveling with the Reed family and slept by their wagon. The Reeds' campfire had burned low, but even in the dim light he could see how peaceful she looked sleeping there. He did not have the heart to wake her.

Gold for the taking, for any man determined enough to reach for it. He made his decision. He wouldn't wake Liza to tell her he was leaving. The explanation would take time, and the men were already saddling up their horses. He would write her a note and leave it by her bedroll.

He closed his eyes. That hurried note. He couldn't remember the exact words he'd used, but he knew he had not explained himself adequately. There was no way to pour everything he wanted to say into a short note scribbled over a dying fire, but he had tried his best. Then he saddled up his horse and followed the men heading southwest toward California.

Pulling himself out of his memories, Matthew shook his head. There were no horses available at the livery stables in Canemah. None. Matthew could not believe it. He had no choice but to walk. He set out along the road back to Oregon City, walking as fast as he could along the rutted track while avoiding the mud puddles. The wind brought another spattering of raindrops, and then more. Then it began to rain steadily. The raindrops beat a steady staccato percussion against the leaves of the big-leaf maples that lined the track. Matthew turned his collar up against the water, but he had no hat, not even that flimsy one Liza had made for him. Water saturated his hair and then ran down inside his collar, cold as charity.

He wanted to race down the road as fast as he could. But this was not a road from back east, flattened and smoothed by decades or centuries of passing feet and hooves and wheels. This was a narrow, twisted western road. Tree roots stuck up at odd intervals, liable to trip up the unwary. Mud sucked at his boots; it took an effort to lift them off the ground as he walked. No wonder most people traveled by river when they could.

The road climbed up from the village, leveling out once it reached the bluff above the river. Here at least there was enough room for him to move at a faster pace without twisting an ankle. He began to run, a steady rhythm. His lungs soon began to complain. He kept going anyway.

When he'd come up the Siskiyou Trail from California, he'd had nothing to show for the time he'd spent away from Liza except for the wedding rings he'd had made for them. His long slog up to Oregon from California had been uneventful until he arrived in Oregon City and had started asking people for Liza's whereabouts. That's when he'd run into Mr. Brown and the trouble had started.

Even if Mr. Brown were truly no longer a threat, there was still the Baron to deal with. The Baron might not have been involved in the attack against him, but that didn't mean he wasn't dangerous. Liza was going to go up against the Baron, he knew it. She would need him by her side. Her pa kept saying that the Baron had a code of honor. Matthew had met captains of industry during his stay back East. They had possessed codes of honor, too. Those codes could get very flexible when the question of profit arose. He could not let Liza face the Baron without him.

Again, as with his mother, as with Vince, he was rushing to save someone he cared for deeply. This time he opened his heart and prayed. *Lord, I could not save them. I cannot save her, either, without Your help. Help me to be in time.*

He slipped on a slick patch and fell, landing on his hands and knees in a puddle. Muddy water splashed his face and jacket, stained his trousers. He was going to look like the veriest ragamuffin when he arrived. *So long as I arrive before it is too late. That is all that matters.*

A strange kind of peace came over him, bringing with it a sureness and a clarity of purpose. All he had to do was the job laid down for him. The rest was in the Lord's hands. He would do his best. Matthew wiped the rain away from his face and went back to running.

The road to the Baron's house wound back and forth as it climbed to the top of the bluff. Addy picked her way daintily along, using both hands to lift her skirts above the mud. Her city shoes were not suited to the road with its deep ruts. Liza trudged along grimly. The wind blew her hair loose from her braid and into her face. It would be raining again soon. She brushed the hair out of her eyes and kept walking. Let it rain. She wasn't going to let the weather or the condition of the road stop her from doing what she had to do.

The Baron had insisted on building a house high on the bluff overlooking Oregon City. She remembered the men in town complaining about how hard it had been to build. They had hauled the lumber up the hill, wagon after wagon, the horses straining and the men swearing. The Baron hadn't cared how the men had to sweat to get the job done. He told the builders the results he wanted, and then he expected them to achieve it. More than likely, this had been his approach to Mr. Brown's deeds, as well. Perhaps he would not care if Mr. Brown had been setting fires and threatening people all over the place. All she knew was that she had to resolve this problem between Pa and the Baron before anyone else got hurt.

When she knocked on the polished oak door and was invited in by the tall and imposing butler, Liza did spare a moment to wish that she'd had time to spruce herself up a bit before coming here. She was at a disadvantage before she'd even begun. Well, it couldn't be helped.

Addy looked around at the elegant vestibule, the parquet flooring and the crystal chandelier, then looked at Liza. "Are you sure you want to do this?" she whispered. Liza nodded. There was no going back now.

The butler showed them down the hall toward the back of the house. The hallway was covered in a thick, plush carpet. Liza's feet sank down into the unaccustomed luxury, and she could not hear her footsteps or Addy's close behind her. She could, however, hear a raised voice coming through the imposing oak door at the end of the hall. The butler, expressionless and stiffly correct, opened the door and then stood aside to let them pass.

Liza found herself in some kind of study. The walls were filled with bookcases that held more books than Liza had ever seen in her life, and the Baron sat at a desk on the far side of the room. Frank Dawson stood in front of him. He was leaning over, both hands on the desk. She suspected it had been his voice that she'd heard in the hall. Frank's face was turned away from her, but what she could see of his cheek was flushed red, and his right hand was clenched. He glared down at the Baron.

The Baron, as usual, showed no sign of emotion. His gaze flickered over Addy briefly, then he nodded at Liza. "Miss Fitzpatrick. Come to play a game of chess?"

"I think there have been enough games," Liza said. "I wanted to speak with you. I can wait until you've finished your discussion with the sheriff."

"I don't think you want to wait that long," Frank said grimly.

"I do not think Miss Fitzpatrick need wait at all," the Baron said. He leaned back in his chair and turned his attention to Liza. He did not even glance at Addy, who had remained by the door. "We were having a discussion of my employee's behavior. I gather that you have been affected by his... shall we say, misdeeds?"

"I'd have a stronger word for it," Frank said.

"I did not come here to talk about Mr. Brown," Liza said. "I came to talk to you about the claim."

A gleam of interest sparked in the Baron's eyes. He steepled his fingers together. "Indeed?"

"I want you to leave me and mine alone," she said. "The root of the problem between us is that you want the land so you can get access to the river for your lumber. I will not give up our claim so that you can build a road. But you can use the ridge to slide logs down to the creek, and you can use the creek to float the logs to the river and the sawmills in Portland. The creek's course isn't as direct as the road, but it still flows to the river."

Silence. All Liza could hear was the ticking of a clock on the mantelpiece. The Baron said nothing. Liza could not begin to guess what was going through his mind just then. All she knew was that she was done with this endless conflict with the Baron. She wanted things settled. Opening up the creek for transport would mean destroying her little clearing on the ridge; that refuge would be trampled, the trees cut down, as men swarmed the place building a ramp to the creek. But she was at peace with her decision. She would treasure the memories and not mourn the loss. Keeping the people she loved safe was her priority, and this was the only way to ensure that no future employee of the Baron would try to put pressure on them to sell.

Finally the Baron spoke. "You have discussed this with your father?"

She raised her chin. "I have his blessing. He will allow this if I ask him to. You know he will."

"Hmm." One finger tapped against his desk. "And what would you expect from me in return?"

"I'd expect you to pay for the use of the creek

and the land leading to it. We'd draw up a contract, right and proper." And it would at least give them a buffer for times when the harvest failed or extra expenses came up. "Also, I'd expect you to give this woman a job." Liza indicated Addy, who looked as if she had half a mind to bolt out of the door. "And to make sure she does not get prosecuted for lying about being married to Matthew."

Frank turned his attention to Addy. "You willing to publicly retract your claims about Dean?"

Addy clasped her hands together. "Yes." Her voice came out so softly that it was almost a whisper. She took a breath and said, more loudly, "Yes, I will. And I will testify about the men who attacked him when he arrived in Oregon City. I saw them hit him. I don't know their names, but I can describe them. Mr. Brown said that they worked for him."

"I do not think there will be any need for making such details public," the Baron said in a silky tone. More concerned with his own reputation being affected, no doubt.

"I disagree," Frank said.

The Baron asked Liza, "You do not feel any need to seek retribution for anything that occurred in the past?"

"Frank will make sure justice is done for what's happened in the past. I am more concerned with what's going to happen in my future. I want no more problems between your people and mine. And if Mr. Brown ever comes anywhere near me, my father or Matthew Dean *ever* again, there will be problems."

The Baron inclined his head slightly, like a king granting a boon. "That will not be a problem."

"Or this lady, either," Liza added hastily.

Frank said, "What precisely do you mean by it not being a problem? I told you that I mean to arrest the man. If you're hiding him on your land, I'll find him."

The door opened. The butler, still impassive, escorted Doc Graham into the study. His face was flushed red, either from the climb or from indignation, Liza couldn't tell. He held himself erect and kept his gaze steady on the Baron as he came up to the desk. "I've come to complain about Mr. Brown." Belatedly aware of Liza and Addy, he took off his hat and held it awkwardly in front of his belly, bowing slightly to both ladies before returning his attention to the Baron. "He's as good as admitted setting fire to my wagon last month. I want him stopped."

The Baron showed the tiniest sign of irritation. A minute crease, barely noticeable, formed between his brows. His lips parted to say something, but he was interrupted by the door opening yet again. Even the imperturbable butler was starting to look a bit harassed by this point. Liza would have felt sorry for him, but she was distracted when Matthew walked into the room.

"Mrs. Graham told me you'd be here."

Liza just stood and stared at him. He should be halfway to Salem by now, but here he was standing in front of her, looking down at her with that quirk to his mouth that had always lifted her heart. "You came back," she whispered.

"Always." He held his hands out to her, just as he always used to, and when she put her hands out in return, he grasped them in a firm, certain grip. Her heart leaped. This was the old Matthew come back to her. And yet, she could still see the new Matthew in him, a man hardened by his time in the mines, tempered by life on the frontier. For a moment, she forgot all the troubles of the past few months and gave herself up to the luxury of being able to look up at him and savor the warmth of his smile. Then doubt struck her. Had he come back to settle this matter with Addy? Or was he back to stay?

Matthew looked past her to the Baron, and his tone hardened. "Where are you hiding Mr. Brown?"

"Mr. Brown," said the Baron, in a clear, carrying voice, "is no longer your concern. Nor yours, either." He looked at Frank. "By this time, the *Lot Whitcomb* will have reached Astoria, where Mr. Brown is going to board a ship that is bound for Chile. He will work on my interests there. He will not be returning."

Everyone stared at him. He continued, serenely, "Mr. Brown seems to have lost sight of the grand scheme that I have for this new territory. I will not stoop to such tactics as arson or murder to succeed in my plan for this territory to become great. I do not need to."

"If he does come back, I will stand up in court and say that I saw him run out of the barn he set on fire last night," Matthew said grimly. He still had not let go of Liza's hands. He nodded at Addy. "I've gotten my memory back, so I know that I never married you, either."

There were a thousand questions she wanted to ask Matthew. She contented herself with gripping his hands tightly. She would wait until they were alone.

Frank said, with regret, "I cannot prove that he knew you were going to be in the barn when he set the fire. All I can prove against him is arson and the attack on Liza's pa. That's bad enough, though. I could charge him."

The Baron shook his head. "Let it go. There will be no more fires going forward. No one will suffer as a result of anything done by one of my employees, even if he was acting without my approval. I am going to be concentrating on politics going forward. I cannot afford to have a scandal blotting my reputation at this stage."

"You cannot ignore everything he's done," Liza protested.

The Baron remained benign. "The only crime that can be proven is arson. I will undertake to provide compensation to the victims. All the victims. Your father will be compensated for the loss of income from the damaged grain. I will pay for the use of the land above your creek, and for the use of the creek itself. I will not try to take the land from you, and I will make it clear that no one who works for

me is to threaten you ever again. My word on that."
He held out his hand to Liza.

She slipped her right hand out of Matthew's grip
and reached out and shook his hand, firmly, once.
Matthew kept firm hold on her other hand, and she
was glad of it. She needed his support right now. It
felt wrong for Mr. Brown to have escaped the conse-
quences of all his deeds. But really, he was going to
pay. His loyalty to the Baron had been overwhelm-
ing to him; it had been the center of his existence.
And he was being sent into exile. He was going to
lose everything that mattered to him. It would have
been more satisfying if he had been facing jail time,
but it was not an escape.

"And Addy?" Liza asked. "What about her?"

"The legislature is planning to move the capi-
tal to Salem next year. There will be opportunities
for women to do respectable work. I will help her
find a job."

Liza turned her head to look at Addy. She met
Liza's gaze, then the Baron's. She nodded. Liza was
satisfied.

Frank leaned forward over the desk. He was saying something to the Baron about recompense for
all the time he had spent trying to track down Mr.
Brown's misdeeds. Liza wasn't paying attention by
that point. She looked to Matthew, who was still
holding her hand tightly, as if he never planned to
let go of her again.

"I've seen your father," Doc Graham said to her.

"He's breathing much easier now. I think you can take him home with you."

"Thank the Lord for that," Liza said fervently.

"We're done here, I think," Matthew told Liza softly. He tilted his head toward the Baron where he stood talking with Frank and Addy. "They'll be arguing this one out for a while. I suspect Dawson would prefer to see the lady home himself. And you and I need to talk." He opened the door and gestured for her to precede him. "Shall we?"

Doc Graham took the opportunity to escape the Baron's study with them. He followed them back to his house, chatting along the way. Liza was grateful for his help, but she wished she could have spent that time alone with Matthew. She needed to know why he had come back to her. But that had to wait until they had privacy.

"It doesn't feel right, Mr. Brown going off and not facing justice." Matthew frowned. "He's just going to walk off, scot-free?"

"It's not an escape," Liza said. "He's beaten. He lost everything that mattered most to him—the Baron's regard, his place by his side. He's nobody now, and I believe he hates that more than anything."

"I suppose," Matthew said. He still did not look satisfied, but his thumb caressed her hand. She could tell that he, too, had things he wanted to say that were best said in private.

Pa was sitting up when they arrived at Doc Graham's, and he insisted that he was well enough to go back to the claim. He even took his usual place up on the bench, though he did allow Matthew to drive. The sun had come out from behind the sunset clouds as the wagon jolted its way back toward the claim. Raindrops clung to leaves and branches, sparkling like jewels. The warm afternoon helped dry the muddy roads, but even so it was a slow journey. The sun was sinking behind the western hills before they pulled up in front of the barn.

Liza helped Pa out of the wagon, and he sighed. "I think that was enough sitting up for a bit. Help me back to the cabin, Lizzy." Matthew went to unharness the horse and give it a rubdown, and Liza put her arm around her father's waist and helped support him until he got inside. When she tried to help him get settled in his bedroom, however, he shooed her out. "You go talk to that man of yours. It's time you and he got things settled between you."

"It's past time," Liza said. She gave her father a quick hug and a kiss on the cheek.

She could not see Matthew anywhere outside, though the horse was in the paddock now, grazing contentedly. On a hunch, she peered in the barn. Matthew was coiling up the harness. He looked around at her. "I was trying to see if I could find what happened to the kitten. He doesn't seem to be anywhere around."

"He was all right after the fire," Liza said. "A little shaken up, but not hurt."

"Yes." Matthew hung the harness up on its hook. He was frowning again. Not the old scowl that he had worn constantly when he first arrived on the claim. This was an absentminded expression, as if his thoughts were on something else. He cleared his throat. "It's still light enough for a little walk. Will you join me?" She nodded, suddenly feeling shy.

They walked side by side through the fields down to the creek. The fields looked different now: shorn of grain, they would rest until spring planting, when the whole cycle would begin once more.

It was the golden hour again. The setting sun reached out to gild the stubbled fields and edge the trees with a warm glow. The air held that quality of stillness that comes in that moment that marks the crossing from day into evening.

Matthew walked by her side in silence. After all they'd been through, to be able to walk together through the fields in peace felt like a blessing. She was content to wait until he was ready to speak.

When they reached the creek, they had run out of land to walk on. Matthew would have to either turn around and walk back or talk to her. She waited for him to make the choice. He turned to her. "I am sorry that I had to leave you"

She nodded. "It hurt—I won't deny it."

"I never meant to hurt you." He took a step closer. "I know I did, all the same. I wish— Saying I'm sorry seems so inadequate. But I am. Liza, I wish with all my heart that I could go back in time and relive all the events of last year. All I wanted to do was take care of you. Instead, I seem to have just hurt you more. I am so very sorry."

She did not step back. Instead, she tilted her head

up to watch his face. "You said at the Baron's that you got your memories back. Can you tell me—why did you leave me, that night on the trail?"

"Oh, Liza, what a fool I was! You scared me with all that talk of six children. I didn't want to think of the hardship it would mean for you. Supporting all those children with the earnings I could make by working the land and perhaps picking up the odd funds here and there from practicing law when I wasn't breaking sod? Not even subsistence living."

"Oh." Liza remembered when she had said that to him. "I never meant… I mean, I didn't mean six children all at once. We could have worked up to it gradually. One at a time."

One corner of his mouth twitched. "Yes, I can see that now, but at the time all I could think was that you were going to end up worn-out before your time, like my mother. And I will never let that happen."

She covered his hand with hers. "You cannot shelter me from everything," she said softly. "Or yourself from all the things that could happen to you. Look at my father. You can see the toll it's taken on him. Yet I do not think he would count it wasted effort. Nor would I, if I had arrived here with you." Then she stopped, her cheeks heating up.

His hands tightened on hers, and he drew her close to him. She could feel the strength of his grip, holding her safe, like an anchor. He did not move, did not speak. He merely held her hands tightly and looked at her with an intensity that sent the blood surging through her body. She had never felt more alive than she did at this moment.

Slowly, he slid his arms around her in a loose embrace, and leaned his forehead down to rest against hers. She relaxed, a sense of contentment swelling through her that was stronger than any ocean tide. This was where she belonged. Not on any particular piece of land, no matter how lovely. Home was the circle of his arms. She understood now why her mother had followed her father so happily from one town to another. She would go anywhere with Matthew, follow him to the ends of the earth and be happy, so long as the two of them were together.

They walked back to the cabin, arm in arm, and stopped outside for a moment. He lifted up her chin so that he could look into her eyes. "Are you able to forgive me, again? Even after all my mistakes and blundering about hurting you?"

"Again and again," she said. "You're going to hurt me, I'm going to hurt you. But it will be all right in the end."

She had been so afraid that she would not be able to forgive him if he hurt her again. Now, everything seemed so simple. She reached up and cradled his face in her hands, savoring the feel of the rough bristles of his emerging beard under her palms. "Loving someone with all your heart doesn't stop you—or them—from getting hurt. I'm not going to let anger keep us apart."

His arms circled her, drawing her toward him.

He leaned down and touched his lips to hers, a brief pressure that felt like a promise. "So you'll marry me?"

"Of course," she said.

He tightened his embrace, holding her so close she could feel every breath he took, the warmth of his skin, the beat of his heart. "I'll speak to the pastor tomorrow." Warm lips brushed across her temple and traced a path down her cheek, butterfly-light kisses that made her feel warm and whole and accepted.

Out of the corner of her eye, she saw Elijah come trotting up out of the growing darkness, his tail held high and a wriggling bundle in his mouth. With obvious pride showing in every line of his body, he dropped the mouse at Matthew's feet and looked up. The mouse promptly scampered off, and Elijah bounded happily after it.

Matthew sighed. "We'll work on that part," he told Liza. "He just needs a little more time. He'll be the best hunter in the territory. Trust me."

"I believe you," Liza said. "It just takes time. And faith."

Epilogue

The distance between the main doors and the altar stretched out longer than the trail that had led her across the continent to this little church. Or so it seemed to Liza as she and Pa started the walk down the aisle.

Every pew in the church was decorated. Mavis Boone had scoured the countryside for autumn wildflowers and greenery. Granny Whitlow had supervised the decoration. Mr. Keller was planning to write a description of the wedding in his paper. Mrs. Martin's daughter-in-law had donated pink roses for Liza's bouquet. Mrs. Graham had donated more roses, white and sunshine yellow, to decorate the altar.

Liza was aware of all the smiling faces on either side of her as she and her father paced slowly down the aisle. But she did not look at anyone but the tall man waiting by the altar. He was dressed in the same clothes he'd worn the night she'd met him, but with a rosebud in his lapel. She wore her best pink calico dress, the one decorated with sprigs of greenery and tiny roses. After the ceremony, they were going to board a steamship and travel down to the ocean for their honeymoon.

Once they reached the altar, Pa gripped her hands tightly for a moment. She stood on tiptoe to kiss his cheek. His eyes were suspiciously bright, but he was smiling when he went to take his seat.

Matthew stepped into place next to her. She took a moment to look up at him, studying him intently, as if seeing him for the first time, standing tall and proud by her side. The high cheekbones, the deep-set dark eyes, the bushy eyebrows, that one lock of hair that always fell across his forehead. Her friend, her partner, her love.

He gave her a small smile, a secret shared only with her. Leaning over, he said in a low voice that held a hint of laughter, "Well, then? Do you know who I am?"

"Yes," she replied softly. "You are the man I am going to marry."

And taking his hand in hers, she turned to face the pastor.

* * * * *

Dear Reader,

I am so glad you shared Matthew and Liza's journey with me, a journey that started with the Love Inspired Historical Manuscript Matchmakers contest. This is my first published story. Writing a novel all the way from the first line to the end requires a whole lot of faith, hope and love. And a very patient editor.

Since I live in the Pacific Northwest, I could travel to the sites where the story took place, stand where Matthew and Liza stood, and hear the muted thunder of Willamette Falls. I even got to try using a scythe! Thankfully, my kitten and I both survived. (Though my lawn is another story.)

The kind docents at the Newell Pioneer Village in Champoeg helped me with details of daily life for Oregon pioneers. The people of the past dressed differently than we do, but the problems they faced are similar to our challenges today. Faith, hope and love are as necessary now as they were to Matthew and Liza on their journey.

I wish you all the best on your own journey. I love hearing from readers. You can contact me through my website, evelynhillauthor.com.

Evelyn

Get 2 Free Books,

Plus 2 Free Gifts—

just for trying the Reader Service!

Love Inspired® HISTORICAL

LIHI17R2

If you loved this story from
Love Inspired® Historical
be sure to discover more inspirational
stories to warm your heart from
Love Inspired® and
Love Inspired® Suspense!

Love Inspired stories show that
faith, forgiveness and hope have the power
to lift spirits and change lives—always.

Look for six new romances every month
from **Love Inspired®** and
Love Inspired® Suspense!

Mason turned, startled when he heard his name being called. "Miss Jones. What can I do for you?"

"I'm glad to see you are walking without your crutch," she said, not replying to his question.

He didn't have to think about why this lady had come. Colton had repeatedly told him that Miss Jones wanted the girls in school. Evidently Emma was a woman to be reckoned with. His irritation over this vied with his unwelcome pleasure at seeing her here, so fine and determined. "I can guess why you've come. But I wasn't ready to send them to school yet."

"Your girls are ready. Do you think you are helping them, keeping them out?"

"I'm keeping them from being hurt. Children can be cruel," he said.

"And adults can be. Do you think keeping them out protects them from hurt? Don't you realize that keeping them home is hurting them, too?"

"I can teach them their letters and numbers."

"That's not what I mean. Isolating them is telling them that you don't think they can handle school. That they are lesser than the other children. Are you ashamed of Birdie and Charlotte?"

"No. They are wonderful little girls."

"Then bring them to school Monday." She turned as if to leave. "Have some trust in me, and trust in the children of this town."

She left him without a word to say.

The girls ran to him. "Did the lady teacher say we could come to school?" Birdie asked.

He looked down into Birdie's eager face. "Do you want to go to school?"

"Yes!" Birdie signed to Charlotte. "She says yes, too. We can see Lily and Colton. And meet other children."

He wondered if Birdie was capable of grasping the concept of prejudice.

"Some children will like us and some won't," Birdie said, answering his unspoken question. "But we want to go to school."

He hoped Miss Emma Jones knew what she was doing. He wanted everything good for his children. But he knew how cruel people could be.

At least no one knew the dark secret he must—above all else—keep hidden.

Don't miss
SUDDENLY A FRONTIER FATHER by Lyn Cote,
available February 2018 wherever
Love Inspired® Historical books and ebooks are sold.

www.LoveInspired.com

![Love Inspired]

Inspirational Romance to Warm Your Heart and Soul

Join our social communities to connect with other readers who share your love!

Sign up for the Love Inspired newsletter at **www.LoveInspired.com** to be the first to find out about upcoming titles, special promotions and exclusive content.

CONNECT WITH US AT:

Harlequin.com/Community

Facebook.com/LoveInspiredBooks

Twitter.com/LoveInspiredBks

LISOCIAL2017